# Fighting For #57
## By Eden Knox

*For the hopeless romantics who also watch sports for the sports…and also for the cute guys. Also, the ones who look at a bad boy in a book and say "I can fix him."*

*To my badass tattooed husband, who puts up with this writing adventure like a champ. You're the real MVP. Love you.*

*To my friends and family who still read my stuff with a smile. I love you all.*

# Contents Include

Fighting for Number 57 is a second chance romance in the Rockville Ice Wolves universe. Sexual situations between consenting adults are described.

Content/trigger warnings for mentions of pregnancy, childbirth, child illness and doctor visits. Please be aware if these are subjects that are upsetting to you.

Reader discretion is advised.

# Table of Contents

# Prologue
## Sami

**Eight years ago…**

A hockey house post-victory is chaotic during the regular season. During the playoffs, the energy hits a fever pitch. Tonight, after winning the championship on home ice? Sheer pandemonium. People everywhere, loud music vibrating through the walls, and drinks flowing. It's well deserved. The guys worked hard this season. Best of all, my brother Elliot and his best friend Kane are in prime positions for draft season. Elliot is bound for the draft. As a senior, he's wrapping up his college career and prepared to go pro. I know something else, though: Kane said he's staying back with me.

There's an unwritten rule in hockey. Sisters and exes are off limits. Kane didn't follow that rule. I'm looking forward to the day that we don't have to hide anymore, but I have to admit, I'm a little worried about how it will go over. Elliot will lose his shit, I'm sure. But we have solid plans. We've discussed this already. We'll finish school together, he'll join the draft, and it will all work out.

I weave in between the packs of sorority sisters and frat brothers congesting the hallway as I try to find Kane. My broken-in Chucks and jeans look strange next to all the stilettos and short skirts, but that has always been the way it worked. Under dressed, less flashy, just less in general. That's fine, my brother is extra enough for the both of us. He shines and draws attention in ways that I never have, and that's fine. He works hard for it.

I pause outside his door, making it look like I stopped to read a text, before sneaking the door open. Rustling noises from the darkness cause me to smile. I flip the switch on the desk lamp just inside the door, and screech as I see two people who are definitely not Kane laid across his bed, naked.

"Sorry, wrong room," I mutter, before easing back into the hallway.

The problem with having a massive party in the hockey house? No room is safe. Note to self, I think, change your bedding before you go to bed tonight.

Maybe he went out on the patio.

Heading out into the backyard, I look around for his familiar face. How hard can it really be to find a 6-foot tall winger with black hair around here? Maybe the hot tub?

I go around the backyard to the hot tub, tucked behind the privacy wall. It was the best investment for the guys, who sometimes desperately needed it to relax after a hard game or practice.

I can see his black hair slicked back, his eyes closed, just past the lattice wall. I continue to walk toward him. He's completely unaware that I'm there, in his exhausted state.

"Kane, I—"

I freeze as I round the corner. He isn't alone. Two girls sit opposite of him, whispering to each other, and one is clearly straddling his lap. I recognize them from the arena, from hanging at the parties and trying to get with any of the guys. I've chased them away from Elliot and Kane in the past.

"Shhh, don't let Moxley hear you, baby," he whispers, barely audible over the jets, without even opening his eyes.

"What the fuck, Kane?" I yell. I can't even enjoy the fact that everyone in the hot tub jumps at the same time.

"Sam?" He turns his head my way, slow eyes opening to slits, before shock makes his eyes go wide. "Sam! What—"

I just shake my head, pivoting to head back to the house or my car. Just away from here.

"Samantha!" Kane's voice echoes across the backyard as I keep walking. The sound of his wet steps slapping on the concrete path gets closer, but I ignore him. I can't. Not with what I just saw.

"Fuck off, Kane. I should have known better."

"I didn't know! I thought—" His words cut off until he gets closer to me, grabbing my arm until I stop walking. "I thought it was you. I came out to relax after the game and thought you were coming in with me," he whispers on a hiss so his voice won't carry. "I didn't know it was them."

"I don't believe you," I hiss right back, wrenching my arm out of his grip and continuing to march around the side of the house and out to my car.

"Wait! Samantha, slow down."

I turn and face him. "I'm leaving, and I never want to see your face again. Ever."

**Three weeks later...**

I'm dying. I'm sure of it. Resting my forehead against the cool porcelain is a relief against my overheated skin. For the last week, I have spent a good chunk of my day just like this. No rhyme or reason. I just feel horrible. A tapping at the door shakes me back to attention, and I can hear someone on the other side of the door.

"Samsquatch? You good in there?" My brother, Elliot says, his muffled voice comes through the wooden door like it has every day for the last three weeks.

The first few days, I thought it was a hangover. After that, I thought it was food poisoning. Now? I'm either dying like WebMD tells me, or...I don't want to think about what the alternative is. I take my time washing my hands and wiping down my face with a cool cloth before I open the door. Elliot's icy blue eyes are half-hidden, his brows furrowed in concern, but it's understandable.

9

"I think I need to go to the store, El."

He tilts his head, kind of like a dog listening for commands. His face is broadcasting his confusion. He's not piecing together what I'm thinking based on my illness.

"I don't…why?"

"I think I need a pregnancy test."

His eyes widen in shock, before he nods in confirmation.

"Stay here. I'll be right back." I hear his heavy footsteps running down the hall, followed by the slam of the front door.

An hour later, and with a grocery bag full of all the brands, I had my answer.

I'm pregnant with Kane Blackwood's baby.

**Nine months later…**

Every muscle in my body is screaming at me. This was the longest two days of my life, but it was the most rewarding. I couldn't help but smile at the baby in my arms, round, rosy cheeks, and baby blue-grey eyes. The head full of dark hair was a shock to my family of pale blonds.

I know who's hair that is. I can't deny it, but I refuse to say the words.

"Hey, Mama, how's everything going in here?" The sweet nurse asked, rubbing hand sanitizer in her hand at the doorway.

"We're good, I think," I respond softly, hopeful I don't wake up my newborn.

"Look at that head of hair! Does dark hair run in your family?"

I shake my head, thinking about how me, Elliot, our parents, and to the best of our recollection, every set of grandparents going back a century were all pale and blonde.

"Must be Daddy's, huh?"

"Yeah," I murmur. "Must be her daddy."

"Speaking of," she adds, looking over the paperwork on my bedside tray, "I see you've left the father's name blank. You're certain of that?"

"He's not in the picture. He won't be in the

picture. He's not good for us."

"Fair enough, we'll leave that line blank." With a few more checks for our comfort, she leaves us to the silence of our darkened room.

"We can do this, Gabby girl," I say, pressing a light kiss to the downy hair on her forehead. "We'll be just fine."

# Chapter 1
## Sami

Holding my precious baby girl is the one thing that usually gives me peace, but today is not that day. We're having our weekly girl's night movie, and I know I'm failing to pay attention. Hot tears burn behind my eyelids, and it's not because my eyes are tired.

"Mama, why are you crying?" Such simple words from a girl wise beyond her years. I look over at her, pasting a fake smile on my face. Pulling her close, I settle her small body against mine and breathe in the sweet smell of her strawberry shampoo. Her lightweight centers me, and the simple act of holding her close has always brought me a certain amount of peace.

"Nothing, baby." It's a lie, of course, but I can't tell her the truth. "Mama's just tired tonight."

The truth? There is an envelope upstairs in my nightstand drawer that I regretted opening days ago. I can't keep living the lie I've told myself to nurse my emotions, not any longer. If I'm honest with myself for just a moment, I would say I've known the truth all along. I knew what it would say before I tore open the flap, and it simply confirmed everything that I kept silent about. I have now refolded it so many times, I'm surprised it hasn't fallen apart. Not that it changes the answers, but seeing it over and over cemented what I needed to do.

Over the last week, I've been weighing out my options on how I should handle the new information. Trevor, my best friend, has been over almost daily with warm words and helping me keep my mind from spiraling. They have had my back every step of the way, holding my hand while I cry, providing an ear when I need to rant.

The results? Her father's side has the greater potential to be her donor. The statistics are in her favor.

The problem? Her father is Kane Blackwood, Left Wing for the Las Vegas Generals, and former teammate of my brother during their time at Ohio State. He is also my ex-boyfriend, but that's a trivia fact that no one — outside of my best friend Trevor, who I've sworn to secrecy — knows about. I intended to keep it that way forever, but knowing that this may help Gabby? It renders that plan completely useless.

Another issue is that Kane doesn't know she even exists, and that part scares me to death. I've worked so hard to keep her away from his rockstar behaviors and the playboy lifestyle that kept him busy in school and made him notorious as his career took off. He was in no position to take on parenthood, and from what I can tell, that has yet to change.

*Vegas is a solid fit for him and his hobbies*, I think to myself as I try to shake the negative thoughts away. Keeping my shit together isn't always easy, but it needs to be done for her sake.

"I'm tired, too, Mama," she murmurs as she burrows in tighter under my arm. Which isn't surprising. Today was full of follow-up appointments and another round of blood draws. "Will you tell me a bedtime story?"

"Always, love. What kind of bedtime story would you like?

"Will you tell me the one about how you met me?"

Shit. I was afraid she'd ask this one. "Are you sure you want that one, baby girl?"

"Mmhmm," she hums. Her eyelashes are resting on her soft cheeks, and even though she's just drifting off to sleep, I entertain her.

"Okay," I sigh, settling more comfortably against the back of the couch. "Once upon a time there was a girl who grew up with a stinky hockey player as a brother." She giggles softly, her face never shifting. "She followed her big brother to school so she could have company. One day, in between classes, she received an exciting message that she would meet a new special person who would call her 'Mommy.' Now, this scared the girl, but her brother said that it would be alright, and he'd help take care of her and the baby. Then we met you, and we knew everything would be okay, and we lived happily ever after."

"We were happy until I got sick, right, Mama?"

"No, baby, never think like that. It's going to be okay. The doctors just need some time to make you better." My heart breaks knowing Gabby feels like her illness is her fault. I hope she doesn't take it like that, or that we've given her the feeling that she's a burden. Elliot and I have done everything in our power to keep her happy and comfortable while she has been battling with cancer. "And," I freeze, wondering how she'll take it. "I think the doctors might have an answer, but I may need to go away for a few days to get something for them. So you'll get to spend extra time with Uncle Elliot. How would you like that?"

"I want him to bring Ronni with him. She's nice, I like her a lot," she murmurs, her words getting slurry as she drifts into sleep. I smile, pleased that she likes Elliot's girlfriend as much as I do. "Maybe I can hang out with Uncle Bishop too." I giggle, wondering how Elliot's gruff teammate and friend would feel, knowing that she gave him the same title as Elliot.

"Sure thing, baby. I'm not sure about Ronni's schedule, but I'm sure Uncle Bishop will gladly come play with you and Uncle El."

"I'd like that. He's my favorite." A yawn split her face. "Maybe he'll take me out for pizza and stay up late watching movies again."

"I'm not sure about that, Gabby girl. You can definitely ask." Who am I kidding? That giant of a man wouldn't say no to her.

Soft snoring shakes me from my reflections, her gentle breaths making the ends of my ponytail dance. Carefully, I stand up and carry Gabby into her bedroom, settling her into warm sheets for the night. Looking at my sweet little girl resting peacefully gives me the strength I needed to fix the issue at hand. I know what I need to do.

I pull her bedroom door shut quietly behind me and head to my room across the hall. My hands shake as I dial Elliot's number. I need to do this, and I was the only one that could. I just needed…

"Sami?" The sound of murmuring and applause in the background made it difficult for me to hear him. I forgot he had the banquet tonight and cringe as the realization hits that I'm pulling him from the biggest event of his year outside of the playoffs.

"El. I," the lump forming in my throat. "God, I should let you go. You're at the gala still. I'm sorry."

"What's wrong? I'm coming over right now if you don't tell me."

"It's Gabby. They found a…" I trail off, afraid saying the word will make it disappear. "I need to go to Vegas." I cringe, hoping he won't ask me why, or tell me to wait. If I put this off, I'll lose the nerve.

"Vegas? Why?"

"Because," a whisper of a sigh escapes me as I close my eyes to brace myself for what I need to say, "because that's where her dad lives."

His silence scares me. "What do mean, 'that's where her dad lives,' Sam? You said you didn't know who he was."

"I didn't say I didn't *know*. I just didn't want to acknowledge him."

"Sami, I don't understand-"

"Just…" a knot blocks my throat. Great, I'm crying, and alone, and I don't want to talk about him. "Can you stay with Gabby? She knows I need to leave. She just doesn't really know the details. I'll tell her when I get back, and you as well. Everything, I promise. I just need to do this before I lose my nerve, okay?"

"You know I will, Samsquatch. No questions

asked, I'll always have your back. Give me a second to get out of this monkey suit and I'll be right there, okay? Do you need a ride to the airport?"

"No, I'll have Trevor take me. Just give me a shout when you're on your way."

"I'm heading to the valet line right now. I'll see you in a few. And, Sami? Breathe. It's going to be okay. I'll set up your reservations for you on the way."

"Thanks, El. See you soon." My fingers shakily hang up the call and start packing. With any kind of luck, I'll be in Vegas  later tonight, tomorrow morning at the earliest.

Hopefully, by tomorrow, this will all be behind us. I just need to go to Vegas, tell Kane the truth, get him to commit to a blood test to confirm he's a donor match, and come home. It couldn't be that complicated. Divorced parents do this all the time, right

# Chapter 2
# Kane

"The Generals are two games behind in the conference standings, and unless Kane Blackwood and his team can get back on track, they may be watching the playoffs from their couches…"

I snort. A bunch of has-beens riding a desk because they can't play anymore are full of all sorts of opinions about how things should go on ice. Bastards. They have nothing worthwhile to say, and I'm tired of them running their fucking mouths at me.

Sitting alone in my house is doing absolutely nothing to improve my shit mood. I throw a bar recommendation at my teammates in the group chat and wait for answers. Going out may help. A change of scenery has to do something for me. If nothing else, it will give me a distraction from the fact that I'm alone all the fucking time. No wife, no girlfriend, and my "friends" are all people paid to hang out with me. It wasn't always like this. I had real friends, and at one point I had a girlfriend… God, that's fucking sappy.

No, I can't go there. That was a suicide mission wrapped up in inexperience and hope. That's for the weak. I'm bigger than that. I could not maintain that level of relationship if I wanted to. Hockey comes first. Always.

Fighting for # 57

My phone pings with notifications from some teammates, and recommendations fly fast in the group chat of places to go. A recommendation of a high-end gentlemen's club is voted on, and an order for car service goes out to pick us up. This will help, I think to myself. I'll forget that I live in a giant mansion with enough bedrooms for the whole team to crash. Perhaps we'll all end up back here after we hop through the clubs tonight, like usual.

I look back at the television screen before getting up off the couch. I need to get ready, but I pause as a statement comes across about Elliot Moxley. I grit my teeth. He used to be my best friend. We played great hockey together, and then I fucked it all up. I broke the cardinal rule: Don't mess with your teammate's sister. There's no way I could still hang out with him, knowing in my gut that I betrayed that trust. So I put space between us.

Could Sami and I have made a go of it? Maybe. She was a great girl, and Moxley did his damnedest to make sure she was safe on campus. He just didn't know that the danger would come from within. And I can admit, it was my stupidity. I let her fall in love, or what she thought love was, when I had no business being committed to anything but my scholarship and my sport. When draft options hit, I pushed for it. I didn't ask her what she thought because to me hockey was the real relationship; it was going to keep me fed after school let out. And then the championship party hit. While celebrating our biggest win, she caught me with three puck bunnies in a hot tub and walked out. I never talked to her again. I took the first team that waved a contract in my direction, the Las Vegas Generals, and I never looked back.

I didn't even tell Mox what I was doing. I just left as soon as I could. The fact that we ended up on rival teams was unusual, but acceptable in our sport. I don't care who is across the ice from me, I'm going to skate harder, shoot faster, and out-perform everyone. I have to prove myself worthy of every single play, and there's no room for friendship in that scenario. So now we play like he hates my guts, and I can't say I blame him. Even just my on-ice and off-ice behavior seems to get under his skin.

Good. A distracted player will screw up 99% of the time.

I freeze as the screen flashes a photo of Elliot, Sami, and a young girl between them who bears a strong resemblance to Sami, with dark hair. My heart stutters obnoxiously seeing Sami's face again for the first time since she walked out of the party. Funny, I don't remember them having another sibling, or even either having a child. My gut clenches as I visualize what Sami would look like round with a child — my child, my traitorous brain tries to visualize — and I shake the thought loose from my head with a shudder.

Whatever. Emotions are not something I have the capacity for and I refuse to let them control a fucking thing anymore.

She doesn't need my bullshit any more than I need that domesticated bliss. Commitment is a con. Anyone who says otherwise is lying to themselves.

Shaking the sour thoughts from my mind, I pick out my new black tailored shirt and matching jacket off the hanger and get dressed. The first thing I did when moving in was turn the bedroom beside the master into a whole damn closet. If I would have had a wife and kids, that would never have happened. Instead, I filled it with suits, custom sneakers, and walls upon walls of useless things.

It should hurt more that I've surrounded myself with things instead of people, or at least make me feel guilty for being obsessed with collecting things. Maybe so, because I don't have anyone close anymore. But I don't have any distractions, either. I have two championships under my belt instead. There's something to be said about that.

It's fine, though. I've learned something important in my lifetime. Things won't leave you, winning stays with you forever. People can, and usually do, leave. If you don't get attached to anyone, you won't get hurt.

# Chapter 3
# Sami

"Final boarding call for flight 468 to Las Vegas." a woman's voice crackles over the intercom. I stand on shaking knees as I wait my turn at the gate, my backpack slung over one shoulder and my fingers drumming restlessly on the strap. Holy shit, this is happening. I acted so fast with booking my ticket and rushing to the airport that I didn't give myself time to register that I'm about to actually board a flight. My stomach is in knots and a headache is beating at my skull, but I know I have to do this. For Gabby. I can't just call him out of the blue. I don't have his number. Besides, this isn't the news you deliver in a phone call. And while I detest the idea of looking him in the eye again, I can't just drop legal paperwork in his lap without having a grown-up conversation first. Good morals are something I've always valued and refuse to let even Kane Blackwood take from me.

The return flight is already scheduled for three days from tonight. Three days. That's how long I have to tell Kane Blackwood that we have a daughter, and convince him to help save her life. No pressure, none.

Knowing that no matter what happens this week, I know I have my family's support is what's been keeping my second thoughts at bay. Elliot has been by my side since day one. He didn't push or pry for information when I finally worked up the courage to tell everyone, unlike our mother. His response was supportive and warm, and immediately inserted himself to help every step of the way. His rookie year, that tiny developmental contract was just enough to cover his basics, but he still insisted on providing a roof over my head and helping with my newborn while I attended school. Even when I told him I thought it would be better if Gabby and I had our own place, he was insistent on supporting us still. I swear, I couldn't have a better brother.

However, he still made my dating life hell. Throughout high school and early in college, El made a habit of interrogating anyone I was just interested in, let alone trying to date. It's no wonder I hung out with him and his teammates more than my own friends. It is also no wonder that the first real boyfriend I ever had was someone on his team and best friend…but I can't think about that.

Closing my eyes, taking in a deep breath and counting to seven usually works when attempting to calm my racing thoughts, but it isn't doing as stellar a job right now. Thinking about the past will not help my situation or the monsoon of emotions that are consuming me at the moment. I repeat my plan to myself repeatedly to help the burst of courage I have from disappearing. With a little bribing and the promise of Ice Wolf tickets, one of mine and Kane's old friends from college gave me his current address. And I can tell from some light stalking on his teammates' social media that they are all going to be out for most the night while I'm flying in. This gives me tomorrow morning to approach him at home, tell him what's going on, contact Trevor's attorney I spoke with while running through the airport to prepare paperwork, and then get back home. I can do this. It doesn't need to be a long and drawn out ordeal where we let the rollercoaster of our past lead the conversation. At least I know he doesn't do commitment and doesn't appreciate what he would refer to as "deadweight". It will make him signing this and me hopping on the next flight all that much easier. If he agrees, he'll do the testing and procedures from Nevada and not interfere with what Gabs and I have made for ourselves at home. After all, his ability to cut ties with anyone and anything was a trademark for him.

Settling into the uncomfortable economy seat, I try to rehearse what I'm going to say to him.

"Hey Kane, long time no see." No, too casual.

"What's up, you disgusting man whore?" No, too harsh.

This sucks, I think as the seat belt light comes on and I brace myself for takeoff.

I remember when things were great. When I moved to campus, it was like I fell naturally into Elliot's friend circle with his teammates. Sure, I was the nerdy little sister, but they still treated me like a part of their friend group anyway, with no complaints or disrespect. They were friendly and included me in everything, like I was one of the guys.

And then there was Kane.

Kane had always been around, even when they were in mites. Elliot and Kane were borderline inseparable, the brothers they wanted but didn't get. He was always cool and aloof with me, but he looked so freaking cute that I couldn't help but like him, despite his attitude. I couldn't help but be attracted to him with his floppy hair, tattoos, and rebellious nature. No matter how much I tried to talk to him, he kept me at arm's length.

Until one day, he didn't anymore. An accidental touch led to an accidental kiss. And from that point on, it was a heart-racing rollercoaster. Of course, we couldn't tell Elliot that we were dating, he'd have killed us. There was an unwritten cardinal rule in hockey; siblings were off limits. He shouldn't have considered me for dating material at all, but before we knew it, we went from flirting quietly to sneaking around at the arena.

It was all fun and games until the final championship game. The after party was insane, and I spent most of the night trying to find Kane so I could congratulate him the way I wanted, as his official girlfriend. What I ended up finding, though, was Kane laid out in the hot tub with three puck bunnies occupying him. I left the house that night, telling Elliot I just needed to escape the crowd. Within the next month, Kane had signed with the Las Vegas Generals and left campus. The Rockville Ice Wolves had courted Elliot and kept him in town. And I had a looming positive pregnancy test.

Even after all this time, a piece of my heart breaks when I think of the heartache, guilt and fear I felt then. I was so young and scared, so new to making my own experiences and mistakes. The pain isn't fresh, but it's a dull ache that sparks without warning. A groan of annoyance slips from me because of the memories, making my seat mate inch as far away as possible and give me a not-so-subtle side eye. If it wasn't for the tender support from Elliot, mine and Gabby's lives would have turned out so much worse. Leaning back against the window, I attempt to close my eyes to get some rest, because I'm not sure how much of it my nerves will let me get after I arrive at my hotel tonight.

# Chapter 4
## Kane

My head is spinning, and I can feel the bass pulsing in my chest. There's a nameless, faceless blonde grinding in my lap and all I can think is one thing: I'm not enjoying this in the slightest. But whatever. We've been here for an hour and I'm getting itchy feet. I already want to either move to the next club or just go the hell home.

Why did I think this was a good idea? I grumble in my head as she once again drops and crushes my crotch for the hundredth time during this one astronomically long song. For fuck's sake, was there an extended version of this or what?

Relief finally comes as the music ends. She turns and drops a sloppy kiss on my cheek, and I move to get up, cursing as my dick grates against the inside of my pants. I'll be damned if I ever come back to this place again.

The boys are all tucked in darkened corners, too distracted by the women at their sides, or the acts on the stage, to pay any attention to me. Not surprising really, within less than an hour of us arriving, most of us had gone into our own areas alone. Scratch that. Winston and Smith were hanging together in a corner with a couple of dancers. Still, we were separate entities.

"Fuck this shit," I mutter to myself, whipping my phone out and texting everyone, saying we should go to another club. I watch from the bar as they slowly look at the group text, making eye contact and nodding like we do on ice. The next club we go to has to be better than this one. We slowly work our way back outside and into the Hummer limo with two extra girls in tow.

"Come on, boys, let's go," I say, climbing out at the valet entrance of another club. We walk past the velvet ropes, flashing a smile and dropping a fist bump to the bouncer before entering the darkened building. The base is thumping around us, the music a throbbing pulse in our bones. Yeah, this is much better. I wave a server over with a crook of my finger and order bottle service for us and head to the VIP section. We're staying here for a minute.

There's a dancer on the main stage, a blonde with great boobs who looks an awful lot like…don't go there, Blackwood. Just because she looks like an ex-girlfriend doesn't mean you should pursue that train of thought, no matter how much you enjoyed her company. Remember. Her brother has tried to kill you on ice before.

Turning away from the blonde, I see a petite thing with a blue wig coming our way. She slides into our seating area, flirting heavily with all of us. She says her name is Sierra or Cinnamon, something like that, and drops her pricing for private dances. Always be selling, as my pops used to say. Smithy runs off with her, not a surprise, and then the blond comes over. The closer she gets, the more I see she doesn't look like… her. Great. I didn't want that kind of buzzkill tonight, anyway. Drinks are flowing and as my buzz gathers steam again, I lose track of my flashbacks. I shouldn't think about Sami. I've spent the last 7 years trying to forget her. Despite that, she was kind of the highlight of my last year of college.

Snap out of it, Blackwood. Damn, I curse to myself while putting my all-star smile back on my face. Sookie, or whatever, doesn't seem to notice my mood change, and continues to pursue me. Whatever, I'm not about to be picky. She keeps edging closer, talking to me specifically. Okay, fine. I'm a familiar face around here. I'm a familiar face anywhere, if I'm being serious. I can't go anywhere in this town without someone recognizing me, which is why I pay my personal assistant way, way too much to go do my menial tasks, like buying socks and condoms.

An hour into this inane song and dance, I give up. I grab the guys and their new "friends," and this blue-haired chick, and head back to my house. This is the same thing we do every other night, and I should be tired of this. I am, to an extent. But the routine of it calms me, and I feel a little less alone this way.

# Chapter 5
# Sami

I look at the giant house on the outskirts, and wonder what he was thinking about buying something so ridiculously big. I know he's still single. He's in the social media press rounds as much, if not more than, as my brother is. The ostentatiousness before me is leaving me awe-struck, still.

I tell the taxi driver to stay put because I really don't know how long I'll be here. Carefully, I make my way up the steps, avoiding the lawn maintenance team, and cringing against the god-awful amount of sunshine reflecting at me from the giant windows. Leave it to Blackwood to own a giant damned magnifying glass.

Stepping up to the door, I ring the bell and wait with bated breath. Is he going to be mad that I'm here? I ring the bell again and try to calm the nervous butterflies in my gut. I'm second guessing all of my decisions up to this point, when the door slides open slowly, revealing a darkened entryway and intricate mosaic tiles.

"Who're you?" a gruff voice slurs from behind the door. It's not familiar right off-hand, but then a wild mass of brown hair and sunglasses peek around the edge. The owner of the glasses and the gravelly voice peeks around further, grimaces against the sunlight outside, and retreats into the shadows.

"I'm…um, I'm here to see Kane Blackwood. If he's available."

I hear something muttered about "puck bunny" under his breath before the door opens further. "He's up the stairs, last door at the end. Just shut the door behind you when you leave." There's some shuffling, and a grunt as someone runs into something, before I hear a "damnit, Smithy, shut the damn curtains! Ugh, it's too bright."

Colton Smith, maybe, I think to myself as I push the door open and make my way inside. Glancing to the right into a large living room, I see the same shaggy dark hair hanging over the arm of a couch, sunglasses perched precariously across his pale nose and ruddy cheeks. Yep, Colton Smith, forward of the Las Vegas Generals, sprawled shirtless across a couch like a discarded rag doll.

Well, he invited me in and told me where Kane was, so it's not technically an illegal entry. I wander toward the stairs he directed me to, tiptoe up the red carpet, and look down the hall. Doors were half open, and I peek in as I pass. I can make out the sleeping forms of random people as I go. Each room looks like a crime scene reenactment, with bodies just sprawled everywhere. I shudder, thinking I haven't experienced anything like this since back when Kane and Elliot had the hockey house on campus. Every weekend seemed similar, when some roommates would let loose. This morning resembled those days so closely that it was like time hadn't passed, that I didn't have a child at home or a few extra pounds on my frame.

There is some noise coming from the end of the hall, a rustling of clothing behind the cracked doorway. I pause, seeing if I can make out Kane moving behind the door. A soft whisper and a giggle, more motion. Awesome. He's not alone and I still have to talk to him. Before they get too far into this, I'm going in, pressing a hand against the wood, taking a deep breath, and then pushing it open.

The occupants in the room freeze, all eyes turning toward me. There was a blonde and a brunette, both mostly nude from what I could tell, sprawled across the top of the bed together, staring at me slack-jawed where I stood just inside the room. Awesome. I can add "remember that one time where you broke up a threesome" to my list of screw ups. Behind them, I notice some movement, and up pops the dark and disheveled head of none other than Kane Blackwood, the bane of my existence and the father of my child.

"Ladies, what did you stop…for," he starts to say as he notices my presence. His eyes widen, blinking fast, and his mouth moves like he's trying to talk, but no words come. Shaking his head, he tries to speak again. "Fuck."

"Yeah, I noticed." God, that was a dumb thing to say. Crossing my arms across my chest, I lean against the doorframe and try to keep my dumb mouth shut.

"Um, Cinnamon, can you and your friend go down to the kitchen and get a drink? I'll come get you."

They jump out of bed, grabbing random scraps of clothing from the floor, and race past me without a word, leaving me in a cloud of cocoa butter. The silence in the room was heavy as I stared at him. Taking a deep breath, I pull my wits about me and say the one line I had been practicing on the plane.

"Kane. We need to talk."

"Yeah, um, let me just get up." He moves, then freezes as he slides from under the sheet. "If you don't want a show, you might want to turn around."

"Nothing you haven't shown me before, but I'm not really interested in a rerun right now," I chirp as I turn around to walk out the door.

"Wait, I don't need long just," he pauses and I hear him shuffling. "Okay, we're good." I turn around to see him standing at the foot of the bed, rumpled pants hanging precariously on his hips, his chest bare. He's gotten new ink since we were last together, but I notice that the Old English "S" that he had scratched over his heart while we were dating was still bold and present, as though it hadn't aged at all despite his tanned skin. He shoves his hands into his pockets, the strain on his waistband pulling lower on his Adonis belt. As if I need that in my present memories. "Let's go sit down out here," he motions to the armchairs in front of the fireplace, and I gratefully take a seat. Walking over to a small fridge in the corner, he grabs two bottles of water, passing me one.

"Sorry to sneak in here on you. I think Smithy let me in and then passed out in the living room again."

"That sounds like him," he says with a chuckle. "He won't remember a damn second of it. He's let so many random people into his hotel rooms that way before."

"That's dangerous, especially as he gets more popular."

"I know. He's lucky it's only been us and the occasional housekeeper." He sips the water, and I do the same just to occupy myself. "So, you said we needed to talk. What's up, Samantha?"

Samantha. Only my mom calls me that and usually when she's disappointed. I'm not about to correct him. We're not here to get close.

"I have to tell you something, and you're probably going to be pissed about it. But, it's important. And I can't apologize for waiting until now to tell you."

"Okay. What's going on? I mean, we haven't talked since what…senior year? Before the draft that year?"

"Your senior year. Yeah, it's been that long." I look down at my shaking hands, trying to get them still. "So, something happened just before you left in the draft. Before we broke up, actually." I look up at him, his dark eyes trained on me. "I didn't get to tell you before you left, but I was pregnant. The baby was yours, obviously."

"I kind of figured. You weren't the type to sleep around." I freeze in his stare and wonder if I should keep going. Then the words sink in.

"Of course not. That was more your type," I snipe at him, hackles raised. Who the hell did he think he was, saying that?

He shakes his head. "Sorry, let's start over. So, you were pregnant. What happened?"

"I had a baby girl. Well, she's not so much a baby anymore, she's 7."

I don't break eye contact with him, daring him to say something to make me feel bad about the situation that I did my best with.

"And you feel like now I need to pay up for it, I take it? I'm not a broke-ass college kid from a backwoods trailer park anymore, so I need to pay up for the last few years?"

I flinch. I wouldn't be the first ex-girlfriend to come out of the woodwork when the better contracts come about. "No, not your money. We're doing fine. Elliot made sure we were okay. Are okay."

"Of course, big brother comes in and saves the day. What. A. Surprise." His gravelly staccato on the statement grates on me.

"He didn't leave me at college and never look back, if we want to get specific about it. You didn't even tell him about your contract before you just disappeared. So no, Kane, you don't get to take that tone about him." I pause for a breath while I get my nerves under control again. "All I need is a blood test from you to see if your genes will help her. She needs a marrow donor."

I've never said it so clinically before, and my heart lurches as I think about my girl back home. Kane's jaw, which had been clenched, relaxes and drops open.

"You've come here, invited yourself into my house, to tell me that not only do I have a child that you've kept from me for her entire life, but also that she's seriously ill and I might be the one thing that saves her? Are you fucking kidding me with this shit, Sam?"

I lean forward in the chair, not retreating from his volume or anger. "You didn't seem to be interested in keeping me around before, so I didn't think you'd want to keep her around either, and I refused to put her through that. We've done our own thing, and you've been over here doing whatever it is that you do. All I'm asking for is to complete the testing for her team of doctors and then we'll go from there. She may not even need anything from you. We just need to make sure that we exhaust all our options for her treatment. Then we can go right back to the way things were. I won't interfere with whatever this…," I wave my hand around his room, "may be. Cool?"

He leans forward, elbows on his knees, and gazes on some imaginary spot on the floor. I'm familiar with the pose. It's the one he took after watching tape with Elliot, or while studying for his course work.

"Fine. I'll do the blood test, but then we're going to seriously talk, Sam. We should have talked before now. I understand why, but," he sighs, "we should catch up. Where are you staying?"

"I have a room at the Hard Rock. Elliot said it was safe and security was tight when he stayed there for the last away game."

Kane nods in agreement. "He's not wrong. Okay, fine. I have meetings later today, but I'll swing in and get the blood draw, and I'll meet you there for dinner tonight. We will talk. Okay?" He gets up, towering over me before holding a large hand out to me. "Let me see your phone. I'll put my number in there, and text myself so I have yours. Fucked if I know where my phone got to."

I unlock my phone and put it in his hand with numb fingers, watching as he deftly types.

"Is…is that her?" His voice is soft, and his eyes are wide as he looks at my lock screen photo of Gabby at the rink, wearing Elliot's helmet and her grin showing off her missing front teeth. It was a good energy day for her, and worth commemorating.

"Yeah, that's Gabby."

"Wow," he whispers, touching the screen with his thick fingertip to keep the screen up. "She looks a lot like you."

"I get that a lot. She has your coloring, though, and your eyes."

He hands it back to me, and from somewhere under the bed, a soft pinging sound chimes. With a sheepish grin, Kane walks over and reaches under, pulling out his own phone. He grins, obviously pleased that he found it, but then scowls before walking across the room to a charging station, placing the phone on the port.

"Okay, but I mean it. We need to talk about this and plan for the future. Can we do that, and at least talk?"

I look at him and wonder if I can keep this up with him. Could we have a legitimate, civil conversation together? It has been so long since we last tried that I honestly couldn't tell.

"That's fine," I murmur, spinning my water bottle between my fingers. "I should probably get out of your hair. Can't expect those girls to stay downstairs forever."

He runs a hand through his messy locks, an embarrassed look on his face. "Yeah, if they haven't left already." He pauses, "actually I'm sorry you saw that. I suppose it's too late to convince you that you didn't see what you thought you saw."

"It's not the first time I've seen that, Kane, but it's okay. It's not like we're married or anything."

His cringe at my statement made me wonder if I went too far, but then he nodded. "Fair point, excellent really. I mean, I should take you to dinner or something, maybe. We need to be on speaking terms and it's been years."

"Let's cross that bridge when your blood test comes back, okay?" I get up from the chair, walking toward the door. "Just call me later." I open the door and notice the two girls leaning against the wall, clearly pouting. "He's all yours, ladies."

Walking outside to my waiting taxi, I breathe a sigh of relief. Damn, I'm glad I dodged that particular bullet.

# Chapter 6
# Kane

Kicking the girls out of the room for Sami should make me feel bad, but it doesn't. Calling an Uber for them without telling them first should make me feel worse, but that isn't happening either. They didn't seem overly pissed about it, so it's whatever. My slowly sobering teammates and friends eventually wake up. I kill time ushering them out into the parade of taxis until finally, thankfully, I am home alone except for the people I paid to be around.

The normality of the daily work around my house, the humming of mowers outside and the vacuum upstairs, is soothing. Sitting at my desk, looking over at my framed jersey from our championship win our senior year. I could pick out the individual signatures, Elliot's giant "EM #68" just under my B for Blackwood, right next to the stitched 5. I've kept the 57 from then, but that's about all. Few of the friendships made in those four years survived the draft, let alone playing opposition for the better part of a decade. The stains of the champagne and beer were still visible under the glass, evidence of a momentous occasion that triggered some of the worst days of my life.

I shake my head, trying to break up that thought before I can dig too deeply into it. I have work to do.

My lawyer's email is on my laptop screen, responding to the voicemail I left him earlier. Of course, he warns me against committing to anything with her without a blood test to confirm paternity. I may have had a couple of concussions, but of course, I knew to do that already. He prepared and attached initial documents for me to protect me against a potential paternity claim, and I'm supposed to be reading them before I go to his office later. It's been years since I talked to Sami, but I know in my gut she wouldn't do anything to put me in jeopardy. I fire back that it looks fine without even opening it. I trust him with everything I am and have through my last few contracts. In fact, he's working with my agent on my latest, since I'm almost up for free agency soon.

A groan escapes me as I ease up out of the chair. I've tried to keep quiet about my knee being a problem lately. It smooths out as I walk it off, so again I just brush it off. I just need to get one more big contract and then I'll be set for life. I'm so close to everything I ever wanted as a young punk playing in rental skates and hand-me-down gear because I couldn't afford my own.

Throwing on my favorite designer jeans and a Las Vegas Generals t-shirt, I prepare for my trip downtown to see my doctor for the blood draw and to my lawyer to sign the documents. I'm hoping for an easy trip and then dinner with Sami. Keys in hand, I climb into my new sports car. I swear I love this one, even though I know I'm going to trade it in on a new one as soon as the new car smell is gone.

My car roars to life, and I pull out of my garage and make my way down the road, watching the strip looming large in front of me. I can do this. I can go in, find out I have offspring in the world, and move on. No big fucking deal. Louie is going to make sure my assets are safe and I don't look like a total asshole for not knowing this for seven years. I've watched other players in similar situations get raked over the coals, and I've tried hard to be above all of that. I have a perfect record. I'm safe as safe can be.

Apparently, an almost perfect record was going to be my average now, I thought with a scowl. But then maybe not. Nothing is official…yet.

"God damnit, Blackwood! You really did it this time," I growl at myself over the radio. My mental berating is doing nothing for my confidence level at the moment. "I swear, only you can fuck up like this."

Whipping into the parking garage, I try to settle my brain. The flashbacks since Sami left this morning are doing nothing great for my mental state and I need my confidence going in here. I'm fine, I'm good, I just need some rest before the playoffs and then everything will be fine. Just fine.

# Chapter 7
## Sami

I couldn't help but smile at the antics of Elliot and Bella on my screen. I FaceTimed them earlier because even though it had only been roughly a day since I left, I missed her horribly. I have never left her alone so long before. It's totally surreal that I'm across the country from her. I know that it's for a good reason, but I still feel like I'm doing something wrong.

"Mama, are you having fun? I feel bad having fun with Uncle El and Bishop if you're not." Her little face fills my screen and her frown makes me lock my smile down better.

"I'm okay, baby, I'm just tired. It was a long flight. I might take a nap for a little bit." Her eyes narrow a bit and I wonder if she can pick up on the fib.

"Okay. We miss you but Bishop says we have to do things to keep Uncle El busy so he doesn't turn into a mopey S-O-B. I don't know what that is or why he has to spell sob, but we're trying to keep him from doing that."

"Good job, sweetie, he needs all the help he can get there." She says her goodbyes and I watch the screen waver as the phone changes hands, before Elliot's face fills the screen.

"Hey, Samsquatch, glad you made it okay. Did the

room work out for you?"

"Yeah, it's great. It's way bigger than I needed, you really outdid yourself," I say while scoping out the suite he had booked me into. Big brother is coming in handy again, I think, because I had him set up my reservation for me.

"Nah, you're worth it. You haven't had a break in forever, and I wanted you to relax and be comfortable while you're there. Okay?"

"You're always taking great care of me."

"Anything for our family. Never forget that. We always have each other's back and that is the most important thing."

"You're the best, El."

"Yeah, yeah. So have you talked to her dad yet?"

And there it is. I wondered how long it would take him to ask. "Yeah, I caught up with him this morning. He agreed to get tested and already had an appointment for this afternoon. We're supposed to talk more over dinner."

"Be safe around him, okay? I'm not going to pester you again about who it is, but just," he sighs, "stay in public with this person."

"I know it sounds like he can't be trusted but I can. It's okay." I look at the time and cringe. "I'm going to need to go so I can be ready for dinner soon. You guys have fun, love you."

"Hold on, let me get Gabby to say goodbye." The visual distorts as he walks through the house, and he pulls her into the shot with him. "Your mama has to go, Buttercup."

"Bye, mama!"

"Love you two!"

"Love you back," they chorused, before my screen went back to my usual background.

I didn't lie, I think as I try to calm the nerves in my belly. I mean, to an extent I do trust Kane, much like one trusts that the shock collar on a dog will keep it in a yard. There's still a small chance that it won't, and therein lies the lack of trust. I do trust that, to an extent, Kane will do the right thing and do as he says. However, I know better than to trust him to follow through on happily ever after like he tried to promise me when we dated.

**Eight years ago:**

"I'm not going into the draft. I'm going to stay here and finish my degree," he murmured into my hair, holding me close as we watched a cheesy B-movie in the dollar theater across town. This was our secret getaway, because no one else on the hockey team would dare come here.

"You don't have to stay for me. There's a solid chance you'll land a great contract if the playoffs work in your favor," I argued. "I'm only a year behind you guys now, so by the time you get settled for your rookie year, I'll graduate, and then we can tell Elliot the truth. You wouldn't be his teammate then."

"I know, but he'll still probably beat me to a pulp." I sighed, knowing he was right. "But I can promise you I'll take care of you when I'm done. I could still get on a solid contract somewhere, maybe even with a minor league team. There's a whole world out there for us."

"You're right. I love you, Kane."

"Love you, Sami. You're the only one for me."

**Present Day:**

I had to blink rapidly to shake loose the tears. Fucker broke my heart, cheated on me, flipped the script, went in the first round of the draft, and never called us back. He left quicker than a hiccup, leaving me to pick up the pieces not just when he left, but also the next month when I found out I was expecting before I finished school.

I shook my head. I swear, I will absolutely not let him get that close again. I know what it felt like to be in the center of that storm, and I am bigger, stronger, and smarter than that this time around.

A shower. I did my best thinking in and around water. Snatching my bag of toiletries out of my suitcase, I headed toward the giant bathroom. I'll feel better afterward, and then I can get ready for dinner. The water pressure and heat was absolute perfection here. It relaxes me, and helps to quell my nerves.

I dress simply in the black slim leg pants and flowy red top that I packed on a lark. Red is the color of confidence, I think, and I need that tonight as much as possible. Slipping into the black heels, I head down. If he shows, he shows, and if not, well, I'm not going to let him ruin this.

The noise of the first floor was just this side of overstimulating, walking into the chaotic press of people and flashing lights throughout the lobby. Clinking from the jackpot machines was still audible. This feels like being in a completely different universe.

I escape the cacophony of the lobby to enter the greater chaos that is the Las Vegas Strip, to walk toward the waiting car. Kane said we had reservations at an exclusive restaurant that the team favored for privacy. I trust him with at least that much: I may not trust him with my heart, but I know he wouldn't intentionally put me in danger.

The car pulls up to velvet ropes guarded by two giant men. I'm not a stranger to huge guys, I lived with hockey players, but this? This was a whole new level. One opens the door as the driver comes to a complete stop, while the other holds out a hand for me to exit. Dorothy, we aren't in Kansas anymore, I think to myself as I take in the entry. The heavy oak door is pulled open by another member of security, and then I'm inside.

It feels like I'm in another world. Soft lighting and private dining areas surround the area, and soft jazz accentuates the hum of conversation between the diners. The hostess escorts me through the large dining hall, placing me in a corner booth in a darker corner far from the major foot traffic.

"Here you go, Ms. Moxley, Mr. Blackwood's private table. Can I get you situated with a drink?"

"A vodka cranberry would be great, thanks so much."

I move into the intimate dining space, the lighting dim and note that we are not alone.

I slip my phone out of my purse as she walks away, and check for a text from Kane. Nothing yet. Best case scenario, he's running late and he still shows. Worst case scenario, he's blown me off and I may have to go the whole legal route with him. I had hoped we could talk this out like grown ups now.

A waitress comes by with my drink, and I slowly sip at it while scrolling through my phone for entertainment. Elliot and Bishop have sent a series of photos of their time with Bella, and it looked like she was enjoying her time at home. I send off a text to Elliot to thank him for the excellent room reservation, and contemplate reading an ebook while I wait. The waitress comes by, and brings me another drink, and I startle as I realize the first one is gone.

"Oh thanks. Um, maybe I'll go ahead and get an appetizer while I wait on him?"

Appetizers are good, they're carbs, and they'll pass the time, I think, slipping back into my book and sipping again, enjoying the solitude a bit. The plot line of my book absorbed me, and I looked up just long enough to thank the waitress for bringing the appetizer platter. He's 10 minutes late. At this point, I'm willing to write him off as a no-show, but I think I'll wait longer.

I drop texts to Trevor, and enjoy the break in suspense waiting on Kane to show up.

**Me:** 10 minutes late, want to take bets he no-shows?

**Trevor:** You're on! Loser buys Mexican, I want dinner out of this, LOL

**Me:** Sold. I want extra guac though.

**Trevor:** It's his loss, you know that right? If he doesn't show, remember I have that lawyer on retainer. He'll take you on.

**Me:** I'll keep it in mind. I'm giving him until the server comes back for my order again.

More time passes, I finish my second vodka cranberry, and send him a text to see if he's still on the way.

I give up. He's not coming, I can tell. I'm sitting in a secluded booth all by myself to eat dinner solo in a casino hotel across the country from my sick child. What the actual hell, Samantha, I think to myself as guilt settles in my gut. Fuck him. Fuck him for being an irresponsible ass in school, and making decisions bigger than the both of us without talking, and fuck him for making me think hunting him down across the country was a good idea, and trusting his stupid ass to actually show the fuck up—

"Hey, sorry I'm late. Traffic was a bitch. Have you ordered yet?" My brain short circuits as I look up at Kane, looking suave in a black button down, with the top two buttons unfastened and the sleeves rolled up, and perfectly tailored pants.

"Kane, you're back! It's been so long!" The leggy blonde saunters over to the table,

For real, like I'm not sitting directly in front of him? I sit and stew, watching for them to wrap up their conversation. Kane is being his usual professional self. I've seen him interact with fans before, and he's always putting the professional face forward. Good for business, but a real pain in my ass for talking.

"Kane? What do you recommend here?" The blonde waitress and Kane both turn to me mid-sentence to stare. "Sorry, but I've been waiting for him to order. I'm kind of hungry."

"Sure thing," she said as she scribbled down my favorite food. "Anything I can get for you, sweetheart?" she says to Kane.

"Same, and can I get a Scotch on the rocks, make it a double. And another one of those fruity things for her as well," he says, handing over the menus with a wink. She walks away with a swing to her hips, and then we're all alone again. "You know if we went anywhere else, she would spit on your burger now, right?"

"Kind of don't care at the moment, really."

"That was spicy of you. I almost forgot how you would be when you were hungry."

I stare at him. "What the hell are you talking about? I'm just fine. I was just tired of watching her climb into your lap."

His gaze doesn't leave my face as he slides the platter across to me. I roll my eyes at him, and instead pick up my glass, swirling around the watery remnants and the melting ice cubes.

"You forgot that I helped take care of you in the

hockey house. You know I'm right."

"Still doesn't mean I need to listen to you about it," I grumble, before caving in and grabbing a breadstick from the middle.

"You always were a brat," he murmured before reaching out for a breadstick of his own. "So anyway, do we want to talk more now, or wait until after I get meat in you?"

I stop chewing and stare at him. "Do you have to be so crass about it? Anyway, where do you want to start."

"Well, we could start with how long you've known she was mine. That seems like a good starting point."

I feel my eyebrow raise at his audacity.

"Really? Again?" Alright, looks like we're diving right into the deep end. "I knew from the very beginning. You were the only one I had ever been with. I intended to tell you before the draft, but…" I trail off, not sure how to proceed. "We weren't exactly on speaking terms at that point, and I had been really hurt. So at the time, going it alone seemed right. And watching you live it up over here while I took care of a small child, it didn't seem like you were in the right headspace for parenthood anyway."

"But you never gave me the chance to participate, though," he retorts. "I mean, If I would have known, maybe things would have gone differently."

"I wasn't willing to gamble on a maybe. She needed stability, and I'm glad she has had that, even with the roller coaster that is her treatment."

His jaw tightened like he was holding the words back. "I won't deny that it's a kick to the nuts that it's taken until now for me to know. If she had never gotten sick, would you have ever told me?"

"Maybe. But I don't want you to think that I'm just using her as leverage on you, we were fine without anything you could give us."

"Sure, Samantha."

"What's that supposed to mean?"

"Who bought your house? Who's watching her now? Who is paying for her care?"

It's my turn to clamp my mouth shut. God, this

was such a bad idea. "It's Elliot, you know that. He has always stepped up for our family." I sigh in defeat. "We can't have a civil conversation for shit, can we?"

"We used to have very civil conversations. I see no reason for that to change just because you don't like your choices being the subject matter."

"You're being a dick about it and you know it," I hiss at him, to keep our conversation quiet enough that the passing wait staff and guests can't hear. "Just because I turned to my brother for support when my supposed boyfriend decided that I wasn't enough for him? I was knocked up with a degree to finish, so I did what I needed to do. Is that the problem?"

He glares, before slamming his eyes shut and breathing deeply. "Maybe we need to table this until later."

"Of course, because it hasn't been 7 years in the making already. What's a few more days." I lean back against the padded backrest, my heart racing in my chest as I consider how this conversation has quickly turned into a confrontation. I should've known better. We were fire and oil, highly combustible and not recommended together. But it was that instant burn that drew me to him even more when we were younger, and time apart didn't lessen that pull.

He eyes me over the lip of his glass, as we sit in silence. Neither one of us dare to break the momentary cease-fire between us, so we just sit back, nursing our respective drinks.

The waitress comes back, places the plates in front of us, swaps our empty glasses for fresh ones, and leaves without making eye contact with either of us. After she leaves, I lean forward to inspect my burger closely.

"Give it here." My eyes shoot up at Kane and I tilt my head. "Swap me plates."

"She didn't really spit on it. She wouldn't."

"Are you willing to take that chance?"

With reluctance, I hand the steaming plate over to him, and he promptly hands me his. He has a valid point, and we did order identical plates. Shifting the fries around to make a corner for my ketchup, I glance at him as he digs into his own food without a second thought.

"Thanks, Kane."

"It's no big, Sami, I know how you are about your fries and shit."

I roll my eyes, but still take a fry from the stack. The dim lights and the rock music make us lean a little closer to each other, in order to hear each other.

"I'm sorry, it wasn't this loud in here last night," I half-yell across the table for him, only for him to crinkle his brow because he didn't catch what I said. I frown, shove my plate beside him, and get up, dropping into the chair beside him. "There. I'm tired of yelling at you."

"You're never tired of yelling at me, Sami, but I get it," he says, turning his broad chest toward me so we can face each other. "So you were trying to tell me about your— our— daughter. Gabby, right?"

"Yeah, Gabby. I still haven't told her why I'm out here. Or at least, not that I'm here to see you specifically. Even Elliot doesn't know the details, just that I'm here in town."

His brows shoot up in surprise. "How did you keep that one a secret?"

"I'm good at keeping secrets, Kane, you of all people should have known that."

"You're right, this has to be the longest you've kept a secret before. So, what does she think you're out here for?"

"She knows I'm out here for something to do with a potential donor match, but that's all. I didn't want her to get her hopes up about, well, anything."

I watch as his head drops a bit, "Fair, because who knew how I would react to you showing up on my doorstep unannounced. Are you planning on telling her the truth at some point?"

"When the time is right. She's got a big sensitive heart, and I'd hate to hurt it anymore than necessary. Plus, between the probability of a match and your reaction, I had been reluctant to bank on anything."

We sip our drinks, letting the silence settle around us. Once upon a time, this would have been a regular occurrence, and there would have been no uncomfortable moments between us. Sipping more of my drink, I wondered if we could ever get back to where we were.

# Chapter 8
## Kane

If I didn't know any better, I'd say I just got ran over by a fucking Zamboni. My head is pounding and my mouth feels like I swallowed my game socks after a triple overtime game. My moan vibrates my skull in a way that hurts worse than before, making me curse again. I'm in agony and there is no one to blame except myself, or maybe that damned ex of mine. Just a simple dinner, she said.

"I swear to God I'm never, ever drinking again," I groan as I try to roll out of my — not my bed. I'm not in my room, I think, trying not to panic. Where the hell am I? Last night's drinks at dinner threaten to come back at me if I don't stop moving, so I slowly settle back down on the pillows. I won't panic, it's not that bad, I think as I try to think back on last night's events.

Muddled flashes of memories come back to me slowly; Sami standing in my bedroom doorway yesterday morning, talking to my lawyer in the afternoon, meeting Sami for dinner last night… Wait. What did we do after dinner? I'm drawing a total blank.

"Sami?" My voice rasps from my dry throat as I try to get my bearings in the dark. I hear nothing in the room except for the soft hum of the air conditioning and the soft murmur of conversations in the hallway. I crack an eyelid to look for her, thinking maybe she's still asleep somewhere in the room. The pillow beside me is depressed, so she – or someone – was there last night. I throw the rumpled duvet cover to the side, relishing the shock of the air conditioner cooled air on my feverish skin. "I swear to god I'm never drinking again."

My head thudded in time with my pulse as I tried to get upright again. At least if I could get to the minibar and a fresh bottle of water I could attempt to hydrate. Swallowing the first taste of water was agony and ecstasy, again solidifying all the reasons I needed to never drink again.

I roll my head on my tight shoulders, regretting not going home to my custom orthopedic pillows. Nothing a session or two with the massage therapists couldn't fix, I'm sure, but it was still an irritant that I put myself into this position anyway. Groaning, I finish off the water bottle, snag another from the small refrigerator, and straighten up to my full height with a grimace.

The pounding has faded to a dull ache, so I take another look around. It looks like a suite at the Hard Rock, based on the memorabilia on the walls. Leave it to Elliot to make sure his sister has posh digs while hunting me down like a damn dog. Dick.

"Okay, Blackwood, get your shit together," I grumble to myself. "Where the hell are your pants?" Scanning the room, I make out crumpled heaps of black on the carpet. Groaning, I gather my clothes and smooth them out on the messy bed. "Damnit, what a mess."

My crumpled clothes felt scratchy and gross on my oversensitive skin, but I only needed to wear them to get back home. Throwing back another couple swallows of water, I take another glance around for any sign of Sam. She should be here somewhere, if I'm in her room like I think I am.

"Where the hell did you go, Sami?" There wasn't an answer to my question, of course, and the more I looked around the more I noticed that there was nothing that showed she had ever been there. I mean, she did come to my house and we ate dinner last night, right?

There's a sheet of paper glowing against the dark laminate kitchenette table, and I pad over on bare feet, feeling the plush carpet against my toes.

"What is this?" I pick it up with numb fingers, flipping the legal sized sheet of paper face up, and then froze.

A marriage certificate. A legally binding document showing that I, Kane Matthew Blackwood, somehow managed to marry Samantha Jane Moxley last night.

We are so incredibly fucked. My heart started to race, I felt a cold sweat trickle down my neck. We're married. I don't even remember agreeing to it, or saying anything. My gut lurches, the legal ramifications of what happened barrelling through my head like flashing neon.

"Oh shit," I moaned as I turned on my heel and stumbled into the bathroom as my stomach churns again.

This wasn't what I intended to wake up to this morning, and I swore as I heaved one more time that I would never, ever, ever drink again

# Chapter 9
## Sami

I can't get out of this airport and away from this God-forsaken city fast enough. What the hell was I thinking, coming to Vegas to talk to Kane? It never worked out for me in the past, the odds of it working out now are slim to none. And to make matters worse, I woke up to find a marriage certificate on the table!

I should have thrown it away or hid it, brought it with me. He would never need to know what happened last night, right? Sure, he's going to wake up in my hotel room, and hopefully with as bad of a hangover as I have. It serves him right, he was the one who kept ordering drinks. Granted, I was a grown-ass adult, and I could have stopped at any point.

Apparently, good ideas and Kane Blackwood did not go in the same sentence together. Ever. Sure, waking up in his arms felt great for a hot second, until I remembered whose arms were wrapped around me and I had to carefully escape the room. Changing my flight was simple enough and if I had even a shred of luck, I would hopefully be able to get back across the Rockies where I belonged before he ever knew I left.

My head was throbbing as I checked my phone for the thousandth time since I made it to the terminal, hoping I didn't see a text message from him. So far, so good. Maybe I could get back home and just go back to the way things were without any issues.

A cheery "ding" blared from my phone's speaker and I jumped, dumping my phone onto the floor. Slowly I bent over to gather my phone from the vinyl flooring, and sent up a quick prayer before flipping the screen face up.

Blackwood: We need to talk. NOW. Where are you?Panic erupted in my chest, stealing my breath and I nearly dropped my phone again. I can't deal with him now. I can't deal with him ever. Closing my eyes to calm down, I open the text message and contemplate the best way to relay my words to him. My head throbbed, making my stomach flip, as I started to type.

Sam:  There's nothing to talk about. It was a mistake to come here. I'm sorry for bothering you.

Blackwood: There is a LOT for us to talk about. Where the hell are you?

Sami: I'm going home. We'll figure something out later. I'm sorry.

He's not going to take no for an answer, I just know that, but I have to try. It was such a bad idea to come here, what was I thinking? I was thinking that maybe, just maybe, he could help my daughter – our daughter, technically, damn that was hard to say – but maybe I put too much faith in his cooperation.

Blackwood: You forgot something in the room. Something important.

My heart stuttered as I panicked. What did I leave in the room? I picked up everything. I'm sure of it. I looked in my carryon to confirm, I didn't even leave my phone charger behind like I usually do. A photo thumbnail fills my screen, that blasted marriage certificate.

Blackwood:  Did you think I wouldn't notice the marriage certificate on the table?

Full-blown panic sets in. I'm screwed. I send a quick text to Elliot letting him know when my flight is leaving, then push the button to power down. Before I confirm I see an incoming call, and with a screech I drop my phone on the tile at my feet. With a cringe, I pick it up, cursing at the stripe I see across the picture, bisecting the last name I want to see — Kane Blackwood.

"Hello? Sam, are you there? Where the hell are you? This isn't funny, come on. What happened last night?"

I curse, realizing that I picked up the call when I picked up the phone from the floor. Before he can say another word, I end the call and set the phone on the empty seat beside me with numb hands. This isn't what I wanted when I came here.

"What do I do now? Shit, I'm so screwed,"

My phone buzzes merrily at me, pauses after four beats, then starts up again. He's persistent, I have to give him that. I look at the screen one more time and watch as the "Missed call" disappears to be replaced by Kane's name again. I should answer it; I should just get this all out in the open. But what if he's mad about it?

The buzzing pauses again and a text bubble pops up, making me grit my teeth again.

Blackwood: Don't make me call Elliot…I know how to find him.

I hit the dial button faster than I could think. Half a ring, and his voice came through on a chuckle.

"I knew you wouldn't hide from me forever."

"Shut up. You can't call him. He doesn't know."

Silence. "You really didn't tell him about us? Ever?"

"I didn't tell anyone. What good would it do? Why would I risk that?"

"I don't know why you do anything, Samantha, including running away this morning. We're going to need to talk about this."

"I'll go back home, submit for an annulment, and it will be like it never happened."

"But it did happen, Samantha. You can't run and hide from your problems, and trust me, this is going to be a big fucking problem."

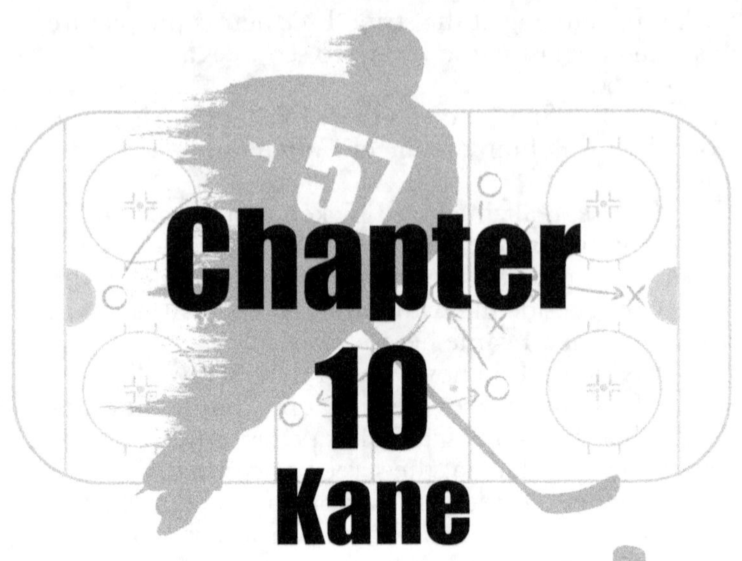

# Chapter 10
# Kane

It shouldn't surprise me how infuriating Sami can be, or that my jaw hurt from how hard I clenched it now. She has always been headstrong, stubborn, so damn independent that it hurts. Helping her with anything throughout school had been impossible. Asking anyone for help must have been torture for her, and I remember how she would begrudgingly accept help. I think it's what drew me to her initially; she was nobody's damsel in distress, she called all the shots. Watching the rookies try — and fail — to catch her eye was entertaining, even if it made me a little jealous.

Knowing all of that, fully aware that I dedicated four solid years trying to prove that my poor punk ass from some trailer park in a no-name town was worthy of her, I still struggled with her today. Of course she wouldn't beg me for my time or involvement. She just dedicated the last seven years being a single mom because she didn't need me. Hell, Elliot probably had to talk her into taking anything from his paycheck because she certainly wasn't going to do it willingly.

Telling her to come back had to be the equivalent of telling a forest fire or hurricane to change its path. It wasn't happening, and you would probably end up hurt for trying. That girl – woman, now – would say no out of sheer spite. I've watched it enough, so that wasn't surprising. How many times had she reduced grown men to tears in college? Still, I had to try.

Staring at my phone, I watched for flights leaving Vegas. It was too late to get on her flight, or even to stop it, but I could catch the next flight there… and then what? What did I expect to happen? This isn't "Say Anything," and I can't stand outside her house with a boombox blasting Peter Gabriel and expect her to run to me. No, she'd need something more than that. But what?

And on top of that, what was my endgame goal? She already made it clear that she expected nothing more out of me than a blood sample and maybe bone marrow. She wasn't looking for love, especially from me. She didn't look for us to rekindle anything or else she would have stayed.

My agent and publicist would have a coronary if they knew that I left my DNA unsupported and fighting for her life in some hospital in the Midwest. I could see the headlines now: I'd be called a deadbeat, public opinion would turn on me so fast my head would spin, my sponsors and team prospects would shrivel up and die. I'd end up with my contracts shredded and that was not the vision I had for my life.

I drop a call to my agent, not really looking forward to how this conversation is going to play out. While it isn't the wildest thing I've been party to, it's definitely one that is looked down upon.

"Blackwood! How ya been, baby?" That thick New York accent made me smile, if anyone can make this right, it will be him.

"Hey, Vinny, good to talk to you. Are you free sometime soon? I need to talk something out with you and I don't think you're going to like it much. We might want to also talk to loop Braxton's office in as well." I leave that statement hanging and wait for the fallout.

"What – or who – did you do? And how is the team going to deal with it?"

Bingo. There it is. Maybe it wasn't as loud as I thought, but that deadly calm voice would get the situation figured out. It's what I paid him the big bucks for, after all.

"I may have a child with Elliot Moxley's little sister. We dated in school, but she never told me before I went pro. She just came into town yesterday to talk to me and get my permission for some genetic testing. I should be getting results soon."

"Did you run for paternity with that, and is Braxton getting those too?"

"Naturally."

"Damnit, didn't they teach you how to wrap that shit up in that NCAA school of yours?"

"Of course they did," I sighed. "I just need to fix this, dude. I can't very well leave her hanging with all of this. The media will eat me alive and you know it. And honestly, I feel like shit out here."

"What are you thinking? Sometimes your brain really scares me, my man."

If only he knew how badly my own brain and my current thought process scared me, too.

"I can't be a deadbeat dad, I know what it feels like to have one. Set up an account and move over whatever child support I should've been paying. Prepare for that part anyway in advance. Give me ideas before then. I'm game for anything."

"Oh, I have an idea, buddy, but you may not like it much." I could hear him tapping a pen against his blotter, a nervous tick.

"Do what you need to do. I'll do anything," I repeated.

# Chapter
## 11
## Sami

I married Kane Fucking Blackwood.

No big deal, right? People get married — and then unmarried — every day. We can make this like it didn't happen. Easy.

My stomach flips for like the fifteenth time as I scroll through yet another search about how to undo this.

Can I annul a Vegas wedding? About 356,000 results.

Does a marriage count if I'm drunk? About 4.6 million results.

Clearly, this is something that has been asked in the past. A lot.

Slamming the lid of my laptop down on yet another search that would take me hours, I huff in annoyance. It will be fine, I'll get to the bottom of this and then I'll be free again. No big deal.

Trevor has been a godsend, putting a retainer on a lawyer for me. She's just a phone call away and then paperwork can go into motion. No muss, no fuss. I still haven't told Elliot what happened on my trip, even though he eyed me suspiciously when I came home early. We're close, but I don't think he would understand my logic for this. What was supposed to be a simple trip to secure Kane's consent and help turned into something way bigger than I ever wanted.

My phone buzzes, and I groan as I see Kane's name light up my screen. Again. For the last couple days, I've had a minimum of three text messages come through. Sure, I might be avoiding him, but seriously, what does he have to say to me now that we didn't say in Vegas?

Kane: Call me. I have a plan you might like.

Me:  Like what?

Kane:  I'm not typing it out, I'm not a dumb rookie anymore.

Me:  And how am I supposed to trust you?

Kane:  I still haven't told anyone what happened. How's that for trust?

I groan, rolling my eyes at his persistence. Of all of the obstinate, bullheaded things he could do, trying to make a deal with me? With a curse under my breath, I push the call icon and wait.

"See, that wasn't so hard," he says, instead of an actual greeting.

"Okay, you have me. What is your deal?"

Fine. I'm married to Samantha Moxley. No big, I can deal with this.

My phone, resting precariously on my knee, lights up with yet another text message from my teammates. They want a repeat of That Night—yeah, with capital letters—when we came back to my place with Sugar and Cinnamon or whatever their names were. In my head, That Night is also followed by That Morning, where Sami appeared in my doorway.

I could never have predicted how that would have turned out.

"Text group chat," I bark into the empty room.

"What do you want to say to the group?" the robotic woman's voice asked.

"Not tonight, I have other plans."

"It says, 'not tonight, I have otter plants.' Send it?"

Cursing, I pick up the device, type the message like I should have done in the first place, and resumed thinking about the plan.

Sami is going to hate this but it makes sense. She needs something from me, I need something from her. It's purely transactional, really. I give her the blood sample and whatever, and she gives me...what?

I could make her come out here and actually act

as my wife. Not in a prostitution way, I have some morals still. She knows what our world is like, and she knows not to get attached; it's more than I can say for anyone else I've tried to date. They instantly see the ring, the house, the life, and I'm not about that at all. She could be my answer to a few meet and greets, no strings attached. The more I think about it, the more I think it's a fair trade.

Picking my phone back up, I find her last text. My finger pauses over the letters, the hesitation shocking me a little. I can't text this. I'll have to call her. A quick swipe, and ringing fills the room. And again. And again.

She's sending me to voicemail. I can feel it.

"Hey, this is Sami. You know what to do!"

"Hey, it's Kane. Call me when you can. We need to talk."

I have a feeling in my gut that she's not going to call me back. I can't really blame her, though, it's not like we're on great footing with each other. And I know it's my fault, but I can't do anything about the past now.

But moving forward, I have a plan. I set up a way to take care of them. I stay in Vegas. They stay in Rockville. Easy.

# Chapter 13
## Sami

I'm going to regret calling him, I just know it. Even still, I press "Send" and hoped my breath to see if he actually follows through.

"Hey. Wow, you actually called."

"You said you had a plan. What is it?"

Silence hangs between us, and just before I'm about to hang up I hear him sigh.

"My day was great, Sami, how was yours?"

"What?" His question throws me, and for a moment I don't know what we're even trying to say.

"Normal people start a conversation with 'hi, how are you,' or something. I'd like to think we can still do that much, at least."

Rolling my eyes, I start, "Hey, how have you been?"

"Good girl," he says with a laugh. "I've been alright, considering my wife left me stranded in a hotel room with a hangover."

"I'm not—you can't—don't say shit like that."

"Say what?"

"Good girl, for one. And stop calling me your wife like that."

"But you are."

"Technically."

"It didn't feel technical that night."

"Do you even remember anything about that night? Because I don't. Do we know if it's actually real? It could just be a fake one, or it could just be the temporary thing that hasn't been filed."

"It's real, Sami, I had my lawyer confirm. You have a certified copy heading your way, Mrs. Samantha Moxley-Blackwood."

Oh my God.

"Please tell me that you didn't address the package like that."

"Of course not," he laughs, "I'm not that dumb."

I release a breath, relief flooding my veins.

"I'm hand carrying it to you. I'll see you for dinner Friday." The line goes dead in my hand.

Fuck.

This may not have been my smartest move, but it's too late to do anything about it now.

Sitting in a private jet, staring hard at my empty whiskey glass from where I'm slouched in the seat, I wonder where this will rank on my List of Stupid Shit. Not as high as the puck bunnies in the hot tub, but definitely higher than "Playing Beer Pong Hockey."

The only people who know I've left Nevada is my attorney and my agent, only because I said I was flying tonight in our latest meeting. I should have called Sami to tell her I'm coming in for sure, especially since she thinks I'm getting with her tomorrow. It will be fine.

"We're going to prepare for landing in ten minutes, sir. Would you like a fresh drink first?" the flight attendant asks, removing my empty glass and straightening the tray table.

"No, I'm fine, thanks," I reply, adjusting to sit straighter in the seat and smooth the wrinkles out of my shirt.

She walks away to finish the rest of her duties before we land, and I consider if maybe, just maybe, I should have taken her up on the offer. It's too late to call her back, so I just sit in silence, and suffer.

The half-ass idea I came up with seems simple

enough. I'll go to Sami's house, present her with her copies of the marriage certificate, and try to sell her on this idea that I'll give her the blood she needs, if she'll come to Vegas and help me. I just have to get her to agree, and then I can come back to Vegas as if nothing happened. Simple.

Landing is seamless, and I step out of the jet and into the SUV I ordered to wait on me. In no time, I'm standing on the sidewalk in front of Sami's townhouse. The neighborhood is cute, well-manicured postage stamp-sized yards, Victorian style street lamps casting the barest amount of light on the sidewalk. Her lights are off, and I frown. Where could she be at 7:30pm on a Thursday night? I allow myself to wander, taking in her yard decorations, and that's when I notice it. The potted plant on her tiny porch, the same one that I remember she had at our house in college, stuck out with its odd position near the front door instead of by the porch railing. How had that plant lived so long? Touching it, I realize why; it's plastic. I poke at the artificial plant again out of spite, and hear a soft clinking from under the moss surrounding the stalk. I touch it again, noticing how the whole plant shifts, and makes the sound again.

"What the hell is that?" I say out loud, looking it over again. Pulling up the plant, I see why. There's a key under the plant. "You can not be serious right now, Sami, what the hell?"

I lift the key out of the darkness and hold it up to the deadlock, praying that it won't fit.

It fits, and I curse. It can't possibly open her house up. A slight turn of my wrist confirms that yes, it does. And just like that, I find myself in the entryway of her house. It's not breaking in if I have the key, right? Right. Besides, we're married, so it's like, communal something, I'm sure I heard that somewhere.

Grinding my teeth, I make my way around her place, checking the locks on the windows and the back door. Elliot is an idiot if he helped her get this place, because I'm pretty sure I could have broken into this place as a kid. No security system, just a single lock on both doors. Sure, the neighborhood looked nice and safe, but come on.

I text the driver and tell him to go ahead and take a break, I'm going to stay put. I sit down on her couch, taking in her decor as I waited. The walls are covered with pictures of Sami and Gabby, occasionally at the rink. The mantle over the fireplace held photos of Sami and Elliot, and in the back was one from the hockey house. I can see myself, sitting next to Sami, clearly trying to look too cool to be wherever we are, but my gaze is clearly locked on her. How we were never caught, I'll never know. My heart clenches as I remember the lengths I went to, leaving her behind on campus and putting as much distance between us as possible.

Pulling out my phone again, I drop a text to a friend in the security business. She may be happy living in a little house where anyone can get in, but my wife and child will have top of the line security. She'll have to deal. Does it make sense that I'm going zero-to-married in 3.6 seconds? No. But I'm not willing to think about what it means, either.

I settle back against the cushions, eyes trained on the front door, and wait. She can't be gone forever, and I'm a patient man.

Sometimes.

# Chapter 15
## Sami

Going out with Trevor and his latest boyfriend was a break that I needed.

Eating dinner with people who do not need their food cut into small bites by someone else is a nice change of pace. Gabby was more than happy to spend the night with Uncle Elliot and Aunt Ronni, so coming home to a quiet house was strange. Trevor, always the gentleman, insisted on walking me up on the porch and waiting until I got into the house before going back to the car.

"Thanks for walking me up, Trevor." I pull the small keychain out of my purse, preparing to open my door.

"Anytime, babes! We need to do this again sometime." He leans in, giving me a hug. "Are you going to be okay here by yourself?"

"Yeah, I'll be fine. You guys have a safe trip home. Love you!"

Trevor bounces down the stairs, climbing back into the car, and I watch as they slowly pull away. As the door closes behind me, I make sure I have the lock in place, and then set my purse and keys on the table beside the door. Then I take a relaxing breath, resting my back against the wooden frame.

I freeze. Something feels off. Something smells off. Like a man.

It's not the first time I've had men's cologne in my house, or smelled it while I'm alone. Elliot has left jackets and sweatshirts hanging on the coat rack before, but this isn't his usual. Stealthily, I reach in the corner and grab the hockey stick I keep there, just in case.

I try to keep my steps light, walking into the house. Looking into the living room, I try to let my eyes adjust to the dark and take in the familiar shapes, when—

"About time you came home. Who the fuck was he, Sami?"

# Chapter 16
## Kane

In the time she was gone, I figured out where the end table light sat. So when she came into the living room, I was completely prepared for the "you missed curfew" reveal. What I did not anticipate, however, was hearing a man on the porch with her, one who says "Love you," especially after she knew our marriage certificate was valid.

Stay calm, stay cool, I'm sure there's a great explanation for this, I try to tell myself as I watch her freeze.

It should be comical, the way she turns into a statue under the light, holding onto a hockey stick like it's a baseball bat, eyes wide, and hunched over like a villain in an old movie.

"Jesus, Kane, how did you get in here?" Her words were sharp, but her body deflates as relief hits her.

"We need to talk about your security around here. Or lack of. Have you seriously been using the same dumb plant as a hiding spot for a key since college? Really, Samantha?"

"Who is seriously going to try to get in my house, Blackwood? Except for you, apparently."

"Lots of people would," I growl in return. "Especially if they know you're attached to not just

Elliot, but me!"

She rolls her eyes, walking into the room and collapsing onto the sofa across from me. "Get real, no one cares."

"You say that now, but…" I trail off. She really doesn't know. She doesn't know that people may be watching her now because of me. She really thinks she's just a no one, average person.

"What, I have nothing fancy. Seriously, the security here is just fine. There's a roaming rent-a-cop and there's some retired military close by. I feel fine."

"Well, I don't. You're going to get a new security system installed, and new locks. Better lighting outside, too. Doorbell camera. All of it."

"Isn't that a little overkill?"

"Not for my wife, it isn't."

She huffs, crossing her arms across her chest. I might have calmed down from the anger before, but that motion fired my emotions in other ways.

Get a fucking grip, Blackwood, and quit staring at her boobs.

"And what if 'your wife' isn't going to be your wife for long?" she counters.

"I want to talk about that. I have a business proposal for you."

"Oh yeah? And what is that?"

"I'll give you what you want if you help me out."

"You're blackmailing me into the samples? Seriously, that's the level you've stooped to?"

"Just hear me out. I need someone for a few events. You need something from me. We help each other out, and then when everything is good, we'll sign the annulment paperwork and go our separate ways. No one ever needs to know."

She eyeballs me hard, like she used to do in school.

"What do you want from me, first off?"

"I need a date."

# Chapter 17
## Sami

He can not be serious right now with this.

"You just flew across the country to hand deliver paperwork to me, and proposition me into being what, your call girl? I'm not a whore."

"I know you're not. And that's part of the appeal. You don't want to keep me any longer than you have to and I don't want to repeat this cycle of finding a girl, agree to casually date, and finding out a few months later that her idea of casually dating includes looking for a ring. You know, Elliot's dealt with that I'm sure."

"Yeah yeah, I'm aware. So you really think going with the girl who wants to destroy your marriage certificate is a safe bet?"

"Are you saying you're going to change your mind and want to stay married?"

"Absolutely not!" I shake my head viciously. "So, how is this supposed to work? You expect me to up and leave Gabby and fly to you at a moment's notice? I have a life here, Kane."

"I know. I'll give you plenty of warning. And I'll cover any of your expenses, babysitting, and transportation."

"I can't believe you right now," I laugh. "Of all the underhanded, slimy stunts you could have pulled, this one takes the cake. You're blackmailing me."

"It's going to benefit both of us, honestly."

"And how am I going to explain this to Elliot. He's going to see pictures, you know. The hockey world is way too small. And he's going to lose his mind, you know that."

"I know that. We might need to tell him a little bit of the truth. Maybe not the whole thing."

"He's going to flip shit. I'd lay money on it."

"Oh absolutely," he chuckles. "I'm probably going to get punched again."

I mull over his statements. It's not a huge ask that he has of me, even if it is just inconvenient. And Elliot would just have to deal with it. I am a grown up, and I can make adult decisions on my own.

"Fine."

"Fine? You'll do it?"

"When is the first one?"

"In two weeks. It's just a gathering of sponsors. Nothing big, no red carpet." Reaching into his breast pocket, he pulled out a card. "Here. Anything you need, put it on this.

I take the card, and glance down at the gleaming black surface.

"Samantha Moxley-Blackwood? That's rather presumptuous of you."

"It's how you signed our marriage certificate, love, so I'm just following your lead."

# Chapter 18
## Kane

I may have made a big mistake. Massive. Huge.

The Samantha I expected to come into the lobby tonight would have worn a simple dress and sensible shoes. Probably in muted colors. Or a pantsuit, because it's not fussy. The Samantha I know didn't do over-the-top sexy, flashy, anything. That Samantha wore Doc Marten's and pinstripe pants to the season banquets. She was a simple girl who liked casual and comfortable.

No. The Samantha that came off of the elevator looked nothing like that. The scrap of clothing that she wore tonight could barely be considered a dress. Liquid gold flowed over her. That's all. Her legs shimmered and the scrappy shoes with spiky heels. I groan, unable to look away from the hem climbing higher on her thighs. I'm supposed to take her into a room full of players and other men looking like that? She's going to be the death of me.

"Wow." That is all I had managed to gasp out as she walked up to me.

And even now, watching her stand with our VP of Marketing, laughing at some cheese ball joke I've probably heard a dozen times, I can't understand this knot of something in my gut that I'm feeling.

I want to walk over there and lay claim to her,

caveman style. I want to throw her over my shoulder and haul her out of here. I want to…

I just want her. And I know I shouldn't because I'm no good for her. I wasn't good for her in school, and I sure as hell am no better now.

"Who's the girl?" My agent pops up beside me, rocks glass in hand.

"No one you'd know." I take a sip of my own drink, never taking my eyes off of her.

"You sure? She looks kind of familiar."

"Just someone I knew before I met you." I'm mentally begging him to shut the hell up because I don't want him making the connection.

As if the situation can't get worse, she walks toward us.

"Hey," she says, sliding her hand into the crook of my arm, the absolute perfect gesture for a real girlfriend.

"Hey, have you met Vincent Moreno before?"

"I don't think I have," she replies, holding out a freshly manicured hand. "Samantha M—"

"You're Elliot Moxley's sister! That's where I knew you from!" He practically shouts at her, pumping her hand. "I was just telling Kane that you looked familiar."

Her smile falls a bit, and I feel a little guilty because she's still referenced to as "the little sister," even when she's very much a grown woman.

"Yeah, I get that a lot."

He looks over at me, shit-eating grin on his face. "And you said I didn't know her."

"Yeah, yeah, you showed me."

"Wait…Moxley, Moxley…oh, you're the one—"

"Shut it, Vinny." I bark at him. The last thing I want or need is for someone hearing about Gabby.

"Well, someone is Mr. Sensitive tonight." He makes a zipper motion across his lips. "My lips are sealed. Sorry, man."

I look around us, seeing if anyone is paying attention to us.

What was I thinking, bringing her here?

"Kane, it's fine," Sami whispers. "Relax."

"Just watch it. Okay?"

"Gotcha. My apologies, Kane, Ms. Moxley. Oh, please excuse me, I should go see my other clients while I'm here." With a nod of his head, he stepped away and over to another group of men in suits.

"That was a touch excessive, don't you think?"

"Not here. We'll talk more later. Promise."

I don't know how I thought "fake dating my real husband" would play out, but this was not it.

Standing beside Kane after Vinny walked away, I could feel the tension coming off of him in waves.

"Kane? Are you okay?"

"I'd be better if they'd stop staring at my fucking wife."

I huff, making the loose hairs around my face fall in my face. "Are you seriously still on that?"

"Until I have paperwork saying otherwise, yes. They can look at someone else."

"Wow. How absolutely possessive of you."

"Samantha, I'm not letting you out of my sight while you're looking like that."

"Like what?" I look up at him, giving my best innocent doe eyes that I can.

"Where the hell did you find that dress?"

"Oh, this little thing? A store." I run my fingers along the hemline, the satiny material slick and cool against my fingers. "I thought it looked like something your date should wear."

"Do I even want to know how much this cost me?"

"Depends. You like it?"

"I'm not sure how to respond to that." His mouth

turns down into a frown as he looks it over again.

"Simple questions, simple answers, Kane. You know how they work."

"I know. I just don't know if you'll like my answer."

I frown. "It was too much, wasn't it? I'm sorry. I should've gone with something more subtle. More me."

"Don't."

"Don't what?" I counter. "Don't second-guess my choices? I did something wrong because you're angry, I can tell."

He barks a laugh, looking over at me again. His eyes burn a trail from the top of my head, down to the tips of my shoes.

"You want the truth, Samantha?"

I nod, concern pinching my eyebrows together.

"The truth is I almost turned you around in the hotel lobby. We almost didn't make it to dinner because I didn't want anyone else to see you in this dress but me. I'm a greedy man, I wanted to keep you to myself." He leans in, close enough that I can feel him breathe on my neck. "I wanted to take you back upstairs and see how that dress looked on the floor, and just how little you were wearing under it." Pulling back, he leaned against the door. "How's that for truth?"

I think I'm in trouble.

# Chapter 20
## Kane

Okay, we made it through the night, and nothing too crazy happened.

Last night almost killed me though. That dress, and watching her walk around, so confident in her surroundings, it was almost more than I could bear.

Not that I have any say in what she wears or does, because I don't. I didn't even have a say when we were a real couple. But what would it have been like if she was actually mine?

A primitive side of me would never have let her out of the house, if we had more between us than a sheet of paper. The things that I felt, seeing her in that dress, flashes of creamy thigh teasing me when I had absolutely no business looking at her like that, I should feel bad. Watching her walk toward me, knowing that she was coming to the event as mine, and leaving with me at the end of the night, made me blood rush.

I shouldn't be objectifying her, but I'll be damned if I didn't feel…things. And I know I have no right to think any of it, but what if, hypothetically, she was mine. I can't deny that I'd love it. I couldn't keep my eyes off of her if I tried. And I did! It was all I could do to keep my hands to myself. I tried to keep it above board, but even those slight touches, guiding her into the room with a hand at the small of her back, just made me crave more.

How was it that this woman, who I haven't laid eyes on regularly in years, could tear apart all of my carefully laid plans in seconds?

And she wasn't even trying to do it, either, which is the worst part. She just did it. No forethought, no malicious intent, it just happened.

She can't know she effects me that much, and I need to get a grip on it.

"Getting a grip on it" wasn't a problem last night, I think with a smirk.

My phone buzzes on my lap, and I look down to see Sami's name on the screen.

"Miss me already?" I ask, blowing right past a proper phone greeting.

"Whatever," she laughs, blowing me off. "I just wanted to let you know I landed. Thanks for last night. It was actually kind of fun."

"Only kind of fun? I'm losing my touch."

"You're ridiculous. So, you never said, when did you need me again?"

Again? I need you now. Shut up, Blackwood, you're not helping.

"I'll let you know. I mean it though, thanks for the assist last night. It was good."

"I'll talk to you later," she says, and the connection goes dead.

Sighing, I get up and walk out to my garage. I need to get out of here. My phone goes off again, and I look. Vinny.

"Hey, man, what's up," I answer.

"He needs to see you. Soon."

"Why? I've done everything you ask."

"You kept a secret from him. He wants to talk."

"She has nothing to do with this and you know it."

"Neither here nor there, really. He wants to see you. Soon."

# Chapter 21
## Sami

So far, so good. No one seems to suspect anything about my overnight trip to Vegas, and no one has caught on about the marriage yet.

I don't know why I let Kane talk me into this stupid thing, but he is holding up his end of the bargain. This morning I received a couriered message with the blood test results. He's a match, and all that is left now is some prep work.

My gut turns a little as I consider I still owe him a couple more events before we can move forward, but then I'll be in the clear. We don't even have to say who her father is, we can keep this all quiet. Just a few more weeks and we can all go back to the way things were before. He can go back to his bachelor life, and I can go back to being me.

The thought has me frowning. I had settled into a comfortable routine of sorts, between Gabby's medical appointments and helping Elliot on the side. But was that all I was?

Gabby's mom.

Elliot's sister.

What about just me? Just Sami? No title, no possessive noun. Just me.

It felt nice to escape from the day-to-day lists. The

flashy car service and five-star dinner may not need to be an every day occurrence, but it was refreshing to step away from all of my preconceived boxes and just be.

Also, it was nice to know I could still draw the attention of a man.

I could have dated previously, but I hadn't bothered in a few years. It was hard enough to consider dating as a single mom, but as a single mom with a sick kid at home? The first couple dates I tried where I had to cancel last-minute because we made a trip to the ER, or Gabby ran a fever, ended up ghosting me afterward. That's fine. I didn't need that energy anyway.

Entering into this arrangement with Kane? He knew what he was getting into, and we had no strings attached. It was a business agreement. Plain and simple.

Would it have been cool to have something more? Certainly. But I wasn't about to push the issue. Not with him. This is a non-starter, through and through. No, we're just going to uphold each other's side of the bargain and walk away.

However, I can't help but consider just what it would feel like to be his again. In the open, where everyone can see. None of this sneaking around, secretive stuff. We started out that way, hiding everything from Elliot and the rest of the team.

Feeling Kane's eyes on me from across the room is a heady feeling, and it was one I remembered all too well. Sitting in the hockey house, in the corner of the game room with a novel, and he would be watching from the other side of the pool table. At the games, just behind the glass, and he was focused on me. He was the kind of guy who would make out with you with his eyes open so he wouldn't miss a single reaction.

I shake the thoughts out of my head. I definitely don't need to go down that section of memory lane.

But knowing that he had those thoughts about me still? That was a dopamine hit I wasn't going to forget. He wasn't shy about sharing those feelings, but he just didn't act on them. His hands stayed in socially acceptable places, and then he left me at my door with a peck on the cheek.

His looks screamed that he would do everything

and anything. His actions said he was strictly business.

# Chapter 22
## Kane

He can't be fucking serious right now.

Sitting in the back of a town car with Vinny, heading to the one place I did not want to be anymore. I'm really getting tired of this shit.

"How much does he know, Vinny?"

He glances over at me. "What do you mean?"

"I mean," I pause. "How much have you told him about her?"

"Only the basics. He wanted to know who your new girl was."

"And you said…" I trail off, waving my hand around to show he should finish the statement.

"I just told him she was an old friend of yours."

"So he doesn't know about any of the paperwork? Seriously?"

"Why would I tell him any of that? It's not relevant, especially since you're annulling soon."

I watch him closely, trying to catch him in a lie. He's the reason I'm in this mess, anyway. He knew I needed some quick cash before the draft. The next thing I know, I'm running bets and coming after the unlucky ones who owe him money. He's lightened up on me in the last few years, especially since I'm a more public figure. It wouldn't do well to connect my name to his business. Even still, he refuses to let me go to just be a straight hockey player.

Once you're in, you're in.

I haven't had to lay hands on anyone in a minute, any more he just uses me as a show pony. Look who I know, look who I can rub elbows with. It impresses his friends and hey, as long as I'm not getting my hands dirty off-ice, we're all good, right?

Still, I'm not happy with the fact that Sami's name is up in his mouth. I should have known better, I should have known I couldn't keep the two worlds apart.

As long as he doesn't figure out about Gabby.

The car stops in front of his casino, and I climb out, straighten my shirt, and walk into the frigid air conditioned lobby. It's like stepping into a time capsule here, thick velvet curtains, plush red carpeting, and flashing lights everywhere. Even the waitresses look like they fell out of an 80's crime drama, in their short black dresses with little aprons.

We weave our way through the crowd, dodging waitresses with drink trays, and approach the golden elevator door at the back. The bouncer at the door pushes the button, and the doors slide open. Vinny and I enter, turning to face the opening as the doors close us in together. I don't say a word the entire time.

As usual, the doors open onto the panoramic view of the Vegas strip, only broken up by the giant mahogany desk with the old man behind it.

Michael O'Connor. Mikey to his friends. One of the scariest men on the strip.

"You've been keeping secrets, Blackwood."

"My apologies. I thought it wasn't worth mentioning."

He quirks a salt and pepper eyebrow at me.

"Everything is worth mentioning. It would behoove you to remember that."

I nod my head in agreement.

"It won't happen again, sir."

"Tell me about her. Vinny gave me nothing."

"She's someone I knew. Thought it would be a change of pace from the other girls."

"Mmmhmm." He does not sound convinced at all.

"It's nothing. Truly."

"So you won't mind bringing Francesca to your next event. You know she's been asking about you."

And there it is. The real reason I'm here. His niece.

"I thought she was away at school."

"She was. And now she's back. She's not the same girl she was before."

The starry eyed teenager begging for our attention and making demands of her uncle passed through my memories. I can't imagine four years made that much of an improvement on her.

"I'm sure."

"So you'll take her out tonight."

"I'm sorry?" My forehead wrinkled in confusion. "I missed that."

"I want you to escort her to dinner tonight. We're having a small, intimate gathering. Family, really. I would like you to bring her to her party."

By "I would like to," what he really means is, "You will do this, no questions asked."

"Very well. Are you sending a car? Or am I picking her up personally?"

"The car will be by to get you at seven."

"Great. Are we done here?"

"Watch your tone."

"Excuse me. May I go and get ready for dinner tonight, then?"

He flicks his fingers my direction as if he's shooing away an insect. I turn to leave, aware of his phone ringing and answering it.

"Of course, he was just here. Yes, he will be your date tonight. I know, but these things do take time, cara mia. He's not an Xbox, I can't just put him in a box for you. I know, I know. I'll see you tonight. Ciao."

Awesome. At least now I know one thing hasn't changed. Francesca is ordering me like I'm a pizza.

# Chapter 23

## Sami

If I can depend on nothing else, Kane's communication will go hot and cold.

For the last week, I heard nothing. No texts, no calls. I thought maybe he had forgotten, or he was done with our deal. One date, and he's out. I wondered if I needed to text first, to open communication.

No, this was his idea. He can do it.

Then the texts came.

First from an unknown number. "Stay away from him."

Four words. That's all. I blew it off as a wrong number, or a prank. Besides, who is "him," because I know many people with that pronoun. Whatever.

The Generals were coming into town and Kane had finally reached out to see if we could talk. Sure, why not. He said he would come to the house so I didn't have to leave, and since he had the game first, Gabby would be in bed before he got there. The plan was perfect.

So here I am, sitting on my couch, Gabby tucked in upstairs, and I'm waiting. Waiting for Kane to leave the arena and come over. I watched the game, and I knew he won. Elliot is going to be a nightmare for the rest of the week. He can't stand to lose to the Generals.

Ever.

A tap on the door interrupts my line of thought, and I open it to a bright eyed Kane. His damp hair peeks out from beneath a backwards ball cap, his dark hoodie and joggers hiding him in the shadows.

"Come on in," I say, holding the door open for him.

"Did you watch?" he asked, grabbing me into a big bear hug like he always did. Surprised, I tried to hold in a squeal.

"Put me down, you beast!" I hiss at him, trying to keep the volume down in case Gabby wakes up. "Gabby's asleep upstairs."

He freezes, looking at me. "She's—she's here?"

"Of course she is, we live here. Where did you think she would go?"

"I didn't think you would keep her here if I was coming by."

I shrug. "It's no big deal. She's kind of used to big hockey guys being around."

"What does that mean?"

His words are harsh and I pull back from his loosened embrace.

"It means her uncle plays hockey and she sees a lot of hockey players, Kane. What did you think it meant?"

"Oh. Nothing, sorry, I didn't mean—"

"You thought I invited hockey players over to my house all the time?"

He at least has the decency to look ashamed of himself.

"Sorry, I shouldn't have— I mean, I should have known better."

"Besides, even if I did, it would have been none of your business."

"I know. It's not like we're really married or anything."

His tone sounds off, like he's disappointed, but I can't quite place why.

"Let's go sit down. Do you want a water or anything?"

"That would be great, thanks."

He walks toward the living room and I head to the

kitchen, grabbing two bottles from the refrigerator before following him in. I find him hunched over his knees, the replay of the game back on the screen where I left it.

"He really made me work for this one," he mutters, watching a slow-motion shot of Elliot checking him into the boards.

"It was a solid game, but your shots were slow tonight."

His eyes land on me. "You took notes?"

I shrug uncomfortably. "Bad habit, I guess."

Shaking his head he counters, "No, I always appreciated your notes on our game play. Sometimes you knew better than anyone."

I sip my water, unsure how to even respond to that.

"So you've been busy, I take it."

"Yeah, coach has had us tied up preparing for tonight. I should have texted."

"It's fine." Am I fibbing? Maybe. "I know how things get during the season."

"We're not even halfway through, I'm so tired."

"Retirement talk so soon?"

"Nah, it's just wearing down on me. I don't bounce back as fast anymore. I mean, I'm looking at a good 3 days to recover from tonight, if I'm honest." His head falls back against the back of the couch, eyes closing for a moment. "I don't know how Mox is still doing it after all these years."

"I don't think he knows how to stop, to be honest."

"Crazy fucker will still play with an artificial hip some day."

"Probably."

"Mama? Is Uncle El here?" Gabby's voice calls down the stairs to me.

"What? No, baby, that's just," I panic, trying to find another reason. "I had the TV on. I'll turn it down, I didn't mean to wake you up."

Kane is frozen on the couch, staring at the darkened stairwell like he expects a monster to come down and attack us. I motion at him to stay put and be quiet, and mouth that I'll be back before going upstairs.

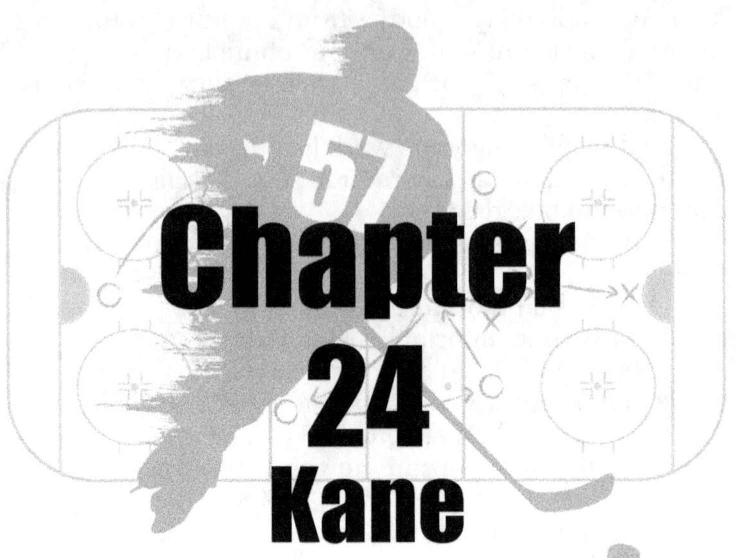

# Chapter 24
## Kane

"Kane. Kane, wake up."

My eyes are gritty as I crack them open, and see Sami standing over me, her hand hovering over my shoulder.

"Shit, sorry." My voice sounds strange, and I reach out for my water bottle on the coffee table. "I just meant to rest for a few."

"You had a hard night. Do you need to get back to the hotel before curfew or do you want to stay?"

I stretch, grunting as I hear my joints pop. I curse, the muscles bunching painfully because I definitely didn't do anything right tonight, like stretch or cool down with the trainer before running over here. Falling asleep hunched over on a couch definitely didn't help the situation.

"I'd hate to put you out," I say, scrubbing at my eyes a bit before standing. "I can call a cab."

"Don't bother, it's late and you're dead on your feet. Come lay down. You'll fit better on mine, but I can take the couch."

"I couldn't put you out like that. And I promise to keep my hands to myself."

She gives me a skeptical look and shrugs. "Fine. Let's go."

# Chapter 25
# Sami

Lord, give me strength.

I can hear him trudging up the stairs, and my heart hurts as I consider how much energy it would have taken him to get out in the cab, to the hotel, up to wherever his room was. He's exhausted.

Flipping on the overhead light, I step out of the way as he takes 4 more steps and face plants in the middle of the pillows, groaning. His feet hang off the side of the bed, and I just laugh to myself. The number of times I watched Elliot come in from a game and do the exact same thing. I don't know if either man would appreciate the comparison, but it makes me smile to think about it anyway.

"I'll be back, I'm just going to finish closing up the house."

A muffled "uh huh," another groan, and then a deep breath, is all I hear in reply.

Downstairs, I double-check the door locks and contemplate what to do next. Clearly, Kane is here for the night. But do I take up his offer to stay in my own bed and not the couch? To be fair, sleeping on the couch is horrible; I've done that before and hated it. Sharing Gabby's bed is out because she sleeps like a starfish, and I'll most likely wake up with her foot under my chin again. Fine, I can do it.

Coming back to my room, I see that he has straightened himself out on the bed and there is a clear 50/50 split to the mattress, and he is still on top of the comforter. With a sigh, I grab my favorite fuzzy throw blanket and lay it across his prone form. I'm not so heartless as to leave him to freeze. Then, I lift the covers on my half, slide in, and attempt to fall asleep myself.

# Chapter 26
## Kane

I wake up in a fuzzy cloud. No, really. There is fuzz going up my nose.

I scrunch up my face and try to lift a hand to move the ticklish feeling away, only to find my hands are numb. Great. No, wait. One is numb. The other one? It's trapped by something.

Cracking an eye open, all I can see is a mound of brown hair that smells like coconut and strawberries. Lifting my head slightly I see why. I'm spooning Sami, her back is tucked against my chest with the blankets wrapped around her like a burrito. Her arms are wrapped tightly around my right arm, cuddling it to her chest.

Memories slam into my consciousness. I used to dream of this exact moment when we were together before. I know it's selfish of me, but I revel in it, pulling her closer for just a moment longer. I shouldn't, I know I shouldn't, but I can't stop myself from pressing closer and just resting my lips against her neck.

She makes a soft sound under her breath, wiggling slightly, before settling back into sleep. Tempted, I do it again. This time I'm rewarded with a soft "Kane," on a whisper.

I should stop. She's going to be pissed if she wakes

up and finds me wrapped around her like an octopus. Even still, I lean in again, praying for another sigh while bracing for an elbow to my gut.

"What're you doing?" she whispers, even as she snuggles back against me.

"I could ask you the same question," I counter as a non-answer.

"It's too early," she grumbles. "Why are you awake?"

"I'm gonna need to leave soon. I still have to get my shit from the hotel and catch my flight."

"Oh." She sounds so disappointed. "Do you want coffee at least?"

"I wish. Maybe next time. You should sleep."

"Kay," she mumbles, shifting again. She releases my arm from her grip, and rolls off my bottom arm, before laying calm.

Slowly easing off the bed, making sure I don't jolt her awake, I make my escape.

# Chapter 27
## Sami

As far as mistakes go, this might have to rank in the top ten.

Sleeping beside Kane was not part of The Plan. Not in the slightest. The fact that I have a feeling that I did…something…just doesn't help.

Calling Trevor gave me little to no help. In true Cancerian fashion, he's doodling "Mrs. Kane Blackwood" and "Samantha Moxley-Blackwood," and designing our wedding invitations.

"Seriously, Trev, what am I supposed to do about any of this? The rules were clear cut. I do a couple events for him, he gives me the marrow we need, and we're even. Done. Cuddling was not on the table!"

"Did you like it?"

"Of course I did, I'm a touch-deprived single mom. Who wouldn't want that?"

"Did he take advantage of you during any of this?"

"Well, no, but…"

"But what, Sami? I mean, at one point, you two had a relationship, right? Obviously, Gabby came from somewhere."

"Yeah, but…"

"I'm not seeing the problem."

"Did I ever tell you about the night we broke up? I found him in a hot tub with three puck bunnies. Three! And he never bothered to follow me, or tell me what happened. He just disappeared."

"Have you asked him since then what happened?"

"…No."

"So how do you know that he did it on purpose?"

"I don't," I grumble, trying to hide my frown behind my coffee.

"I want you to do something. Don't give me that look." He points a finger at me. "I want you to start a heart to heart with him. I mean, you two have a child together, and paperwork binding you. Before you undo all of it, talk!"

I shake my head.

"It's been so long, I don't know if we can start over. And besides, he's established in Vegas and I'm…here."

"So? What's saying he can't come here?"

"A 3 year, $35mil contract with the Generals, according to reporters." I shrug. "I guess technically he hasn't signed yet, but there's no way he'll pass that up."

"Okay, fine, the sportsball rules…rule," he snarks, with a look. "But what's saying you can't go there?"

"All of Gabby's specialists are here, Elliot is here to provide backup assistance, we're established here."

"Damn, Sami, why do you have to bust my romantic bubble? You need to be happy. Scratch that, you deserve to be happy. If he's the one that does it, you should be together."

"But I don't know if he is the one that would make me happy. I mean, the last time we tried to talk about being together, he disappeared, signed a contract with Vegas, and went radio silent. And now that we have this," I look around before whispering, "marriage certificate." I shake my head. "It can disappear as easily as it appeared, so I refuse to think about it too hard."

"People change, you know that. You've changed, I've changed, he's probably changed a lot as well. See what an older, wiser Kane Blackwood is like before you write him off, okay?"

"Fine, I'll hear him out," I grumble, feeling my

hard-won determination crumbling beneath me.

# Chapter 28
## Kane

Waking up alone now doesn't have the same feeling as before. I used to love it. Knowing there was no one there to expect me to be "on" from day one. It's why I never usually let anyone sleep over before. But now, after waking up wrapped up in Sami, I don't want to wake up alone again.

It's not a good feeling for someone who is actively trying to stay away from her.

I trudge into my kitchen, ready to brew some coffee, and freeze at the bottom of the stairs as I smell coffee already brewing. No one should be here, I didn't bring anyone home last night. Not even my friends on the team. So who made me coffee?

Snippets of conversation between a man and a woman drift to me, but not enough to hear who it is. My teeth grind, and I mentally prepare myself for a confrontation. Slowly, I step toward the kitchen door until—

"Vinny, how long are you going to let him sleep up there? I need to talk to him. Now."

Vinny, and who? Francesca?

I roll my eyes, because entertaining her is not on my to-do list today. Hell, it's not on my to-do list for any day. I'm not paid enough to entertain someone who thinks they are entitled to another person. Ever. No amount of money or power should give you the supposed right to another person, and since she uses her position with her uncle to get access to me? Yeah, no thanks.

She's made it clear why she wants me, but she's also not listening when I say no, either. She's not my type.

Taking a deep, fortifying breath, I walk into the kitchen.

"Vinny, you're here early. And you brought a friend."

"Baby, I missed you," she coos, coming around the island to hug me. I hold out a hand to stop her.

"Why are you here, Francesca?"

"I wanted to see you," she pouted. "You didn't answer your phone. When Vinny came to see Uncle Mikey, I said I wanted to come along to check on you."

I look at Vinny, my face clearly saying "What the fuck, dude?" He just shrugs his shoulders back at me.

"You know how he is, Kane. I didn't have a lot of say in the matter."

I shake my head. "Yeah, I'm gonna need you both to go. Sorry, but no. You don't just get to drop in on me like this."

Her face drops, the impeccable, smiling mask falling to show me the true icy look.

"My uncle will hear about this."

"I'm sure he will. Call next time, and wait for an answer. Don't just show up."

With a stamp of her foot, she headed toward the door, Vinny slowly following behind her.

"I'll call you later, okay?" I say to him softly. I can't blame him for this, I know his hands are usually tied.

He nods, then follows her out. She screeches from the door for him to hurry up, and all I can think is I've dodged a bullet with this one.

# Chapter 29
## Sami

Going into Vegas feels different this time. Sure, we've talked about how we can't do anything dumb like sleeping in the same bed together again, but I can still feel a tension that wasn't there before. Also, why am I so disappointed that I won't wake up in his arms again?

Girl, get a grip, I tell myself for the umpteenth time since boarding the plane. We've tried that relationship thing before and it wasn't pretty, or cute. It was a disaster. It was a solid one-star experience, do not recommend. Just because he's older, tattooed, and I'm in a dry spell does not justify considering anything.

Although, would it be so bad to blow off some steam with him? No promises. Just sex. He's not bad at it, and I know he's good at the no strings attached thing.

Walking out into the dry Vegas heat, I look for the driver with my name card, like last time. No one is waiting for me, I realize on a sigh. Cool. Fine, thanks, Kane. I pull out my phone, intending to call my own Uber.

Kane: Look to your left.

I scowl at my phone. What is he talking about? I look left, and see him standing beside a silver sports car, dark aviators glinting in the sun. The corner of his mouth kicks up, and he motions me over with two fingers. The breath wooshes out of my lungs, because no matter how pissed I am at him, that look just does…something to me.

"Hey, how was your flight?" he asks casually as he snags the handle of my suitcase, opening the passenger door for me before storing it in the trunk.

"It was decent, thanks," I respond as I turn to get in the car, closing the door behind me.

He slides into the driver's seat, his large form taking up more of the space than he should. His hand reaches between us to the gear shift, and he deftly moves his car back into the flow of traffic. It's not the first time that we've sat like this, but this time feels different. Pulling onto the freeway, his pinky brushes my thigh as he shifts into fifth gear. I gasp involuntarily at the shock of the touch, my heart racing. What the hell is wrong with you, I admonish as I shift in the seat to give him more room.

"Sorry," he mutters, taking his hand off the shifter and dropping his arm onto his thigh, flipping his hand over to cup the bottom of the steering wheel instead of his left hand.

"It's okay."

"So," he starts, "about tonight."

"What about it? Same as before, right? We go, you talk to people, we make the rounds, we go our separate ways. I got it."

"It's not as simple as all that." He pauses, looking over at me as he pulls up to a red light.

"What do you have me roped into this time."

"It's a bit more…intimate than that." His eyes are locked on me and I don't know what to make of it.

"Like…" I wave my hand, motioning for him to keep going.

"Like, it may actually be a real date. Not an event."

I stare at him in disbelief.

"Are you serious with me right now?"

"I didn't know if you'd agree to it without something attached. I just," he trails off, accelerating through the green light and fighting for words, "I just wanted to take you on a proper date. No ulterior motives, just us. And food. That's all."

"You're so fucking ridiculous, Kane." I shoot him a dark look as he pulls up to my hotel. "So what's the dress code?"

"I left something in your room for you. Don't be mad, I just…I wanted to do it."

"Fine, I'll go with it. When are you coming back to get me?"

"Can I pick you up at 7?" He pulls up to the entrance of the hotel, locking eyes with me and holding a card between his thick fingers. "Here's your room key."

"Thanks. I guess I'll see you in a bit." Before he can respond, I'm climbing out of the car, waiting for him to release my bag.

"Hey, wait," he says, climbing out from the driver's side to come around, grabbing my bag before I can. "Let me at least get this inside for you?"

"Kane, I'm a big girl, and I carried that bag all the way through the airport by myself. It's fine. I'll see you at 7."

Taking my bag from his hands, I head inside, wondering what in the hell he has planned for us.

I should have known he would have impeccable taste. A tasteful black dress, exactly my size, laying across the foot of the bed, with a gleaming black shoe box on top, caught my attention as I walked in.

Settling into my room, I tried to ignore their presence. Good luck with that, I think, as I head to the bathroom. A shower, then prepping my hair should keep me occupied and not thinking about what That Dress might mean.

It's just dinner, I tell myself, as I get ready. I let the hot water beat the tension out of my tight shoulders, mentally preparing myself for whatever he has planned for tonight. I'm so wrapped up in the details, my head spinning with ideas.

There's a knock at the door, and I scream, nearly

poking my eye with my eyeliner. Cursing, I grab a makeup wipe to try and salvage my face as I walk to the door. Peeking through the peephole I curse, seeing Kane. He's decked out in black slacks and a white button down, sleeves rolled up to his elbows. I open the door a crack so he can come in, and head back to the bathroom, not even bothering to close the door behind me.

"Hey, are you almost– what are you doing?"

"Fixing my makeup. You scared the daylights out of me, I hope you know."

"Sorry, I know I'm a little early but– can I help? You have a little…" He reaches over, taking the cloth from my hand.

I freeze, feeling his free hand hold onto my chin and tilt my head back a bit. My eyelids drift shut, and I feel the cool edge of the damp material against my cheek. Gently, so lightly I barely feel it, he wipes away the extra makeup.

"That's better," he whispers, his breath gliding across my eyelashes.

I let my eyes open, and see his eyes laser focused on me. It's not an unusual look, I've seen him look like that during faceoffs more than once. However, to see that intent, that concentration, completely zeroed in on me. His thumb comes up, running softly along my unpainted bottom lip. A soft gasp escapes my lips, and I watch his own lip suck in between his teeth.

"Kane," I whisper.

"Yeah," he whispers back, still not moving.

"I need to finish getting ready, don't you think?"

It's like I've punched him in the gut.

"What? Oh, um, yeah. Sorry," he stammers, stepping back away from me. Turning away from me, he walks into the kitchenette, grabbing a bottle of water. "Take your time."

I walk back into the bathroom on shaky legs, looking to salvage what I'd started on my face.

"I'm ready," I say, emerging from the room a few minutes later. He looks over at me from the counter, his head lowered.

"Sweet, let's go." He stalks over looking me up and

down. "You look amazing. I didn't get to tell you earlier."

"Thanks. You look great too," I respond, feeling my cheeks heat under his gaze.

We drive in near silence to a restaurant on the outskirts, with no windows and intimate booths. I can feel his eyes on me the entire time I'm getting situated, and he slides in beside me. The tension between us is nearly palpable. He's tense, his bunching in his forearms as he tries not to drum his fingers on the table.

"Kane, we don't have to…"

"Sami, I want to. I just," he sighs. "I don't want to fuck this up and I'm bound to."

"I seriously doubt it, you're overthinking this." I rest my hand on his forearm. "It's just dinner, after all."

He visibly relaxes a bit, and runs his hand over top of where my hand lays on him.

"You're right. We used to do this all the damn time."

I laugh. "Exactly."

I take a sip of my wine, and we ease into conversation between bites. This was what he wanted and tried so hard to accomplish. Perhaps, in a different timeline, this would have been us. Freshly graduated from college, settling into his first team, and making a home together. Do we have a chance to pick back up where we left off? Would I want that? I couldn't deny that I enjoyed our time together in a way that I hadn't experienced elsewhere.

"Sami, I–"

"Oh, Kane, I didn't know you were going to be here. Who's your friend?"

We both look up, seeing a tall woman with long black hair pulled into a sleek ponytail, arms crossed, and tapping her heel as she looked down on our table.

"What the…" Kane starts, but she interrupts him.

"Now, Kane, where are your manners?" She holds out a manicured hand to me, her smile cool and calculating. "Hi, I'm Francesca. Did he tell you we were dating?"

# Chapter 30
# Kane

I swear to god I think I'm going to puke.

Francesca is standing by the table, grinning like a damn idiot at Sami. To be fair, Sami is holding it together decently. I would have gotten up and punched someone who interrupted my date if I was her.

I clear my throat. "Francesca, what are–"

"Uncle Mikey couldn't get through to you for dinner tonight, so I almost had to come by myself," she says, tightening her lips into a little pout. "Thankfully he said I could meet him here, but then I saw you over here, and thought 'why not just come and say hi?'"

"Okay. You came over and said 'hi.' You can go now." I start. "You wouldn't want to keep him waiting."

"I'm not keeping him waiting. I sent a message to him already. Oh, that means he also knows that my boyfriend is on a date with another woman."

Sami gasps softly at the boyfriend title. I clench my jaw, holding back the urge to scream at her that I'm not her boyfriend, that I never have been and never will.

"Oh Jesus Christ," I mutter under my breath. I'll never hear the end of this.

I glance over at Sami, my gut clenching as I take in her appearance. She's pale, her lips pressed in a thin line, eyes wide. She's trying so hard to keep her shit together. I have to get her out of here, away from Francesca.

"Sami, I–"

"Let's just go," she says, gathering her purse up. Pasting a fake smile on her face, she mutters, "Nice to meet you."

"Oh, leaving so soon?" Francesca's saccharine tone cuts through our conversation.

"Yeah," I say. "The food is a little off tonight. You have a good evening, though." Never let it be said that I have shit manners. I can hold it all together when I want to.

"Too bad," she says on a frown. "I'll see you soon, Kane." With a wave of her fingers, she turns her back on us and the destruction she's leaving behind.

"I'll take you back to the hotel." I say softly to Sami, holding my hand out to her.

"No. Not the hotel."

"My place okay?"

"Perfect. Just get us away from here."

# Chapter 31
## Sami

She's standing by the large windows looking over the city skyline, a glass of wine in her hand. The light from the kitchen is throwing shadows across her, but I think I can catch a sparkle on her cheek.

She's crying. This strong, beautiful woman is breaking in my living room.

"Samantha," I call to her softly, walking up to her. "Hey, come here." I carefully take the glass from her trembling hands, setting it on the bookcase by the window before folding her into my arms. I've done this countless times in the past, but this felt different. We both need this, I think to myself, as I slide my hands up and down her spine, trying to give her some kind of comfort.

I can feel her sob as her arms wrap around me, holding me tighter. I feel helpless as she breaks down, her tears soaking into my shirt. I whisper nonsense into her hair, trying anything to make her feel better. God, I always was a sucker for her tears. It didn't matter how big or small the situation was, I couldn't take it, and would do anything in my power to make her stop.

Anything. Of all the times for a flashback, remembering the time her final paper disappeared on her hard drive and she bawled in my dorm room. My eyes slam shut and I try to block out the visual of me railing her speechless before running to the library for her books again, buying her a gallon of coffee, and then staying up with her all night while she rebuilt everything with a day to spare before her due date. This scenario feels eerily close to that one, and I fight to hold back a groan as she pulls herself closer to me, her breasts pressing into my chest.

Don't be a neanderthal, Blackwood, she's upset.

"Talk to me, Samantha, what do you need from me? How can I help?"

She shakes her head against my neck. "It's just hard keeping a positive face up." She sniffs, the sound twisting my gut. "I'm sorry, you don't have to do anything, I'll be fine. I don't know why it's bothering me so much that someone had a relationship with you before now, I don't own you. I'll be fine."

"We haven't. We didn't— I mean, there's no history there."

Her head lifts, eyes locked on mine. "What do you mean?"

"I mean," I pause, shifting her in my hold so I could look her in the face, "I know her uncle. He asked me to take her around to a couple parties but that's all. I've never been alone with her ever."

"You don't have to do this, Kane, you don't have to explain everything away."

"I'm aware of that, Samantha. Try again. What. Do. You. Need."

"I can't…You can't seriously be considering…" She trails off, leaving the sentence unfinished as she shakes her head. "Kane, why?"

"You need it. I'm here. We can compartmentalize this any way you want. Just physical, just filling a need. No titles, no feelings. Take it out on me."

"You're serious," she whispers, her wide eyes never leaving my face.

"If it distracts you so you can focus, then let's go. Whenever, wherever. We can even discuss however you want if you need."

"You've hit your head too many times, Blackwood," she says on a laugh.

Fighting for # 57

"Samantha, I can confirm I'm serious, and I've only been in concussion protocol once."

There's a tentative smile on her face, but I just can't stop myself. I lean in, pressing a soft kiss against her lips, waiting for her to react. Just like she had countless times before on campus, a soft moan escaped her before she slid her hands up my chest to wrap around my neck.

It was like coming home again. I groaned against her lips, pulling her tight against me, letting her feel exactly what I thought.

"Just this once," she mumbles against my lips, sliding her fingernails along my scalp, tugging lightly on my hair. Maybe I'm not the only one who remembers how good we were together.

Before she can change her mind, I pick her up by her thighs, her legs wrapping around my waist, and I start walking us to my room.

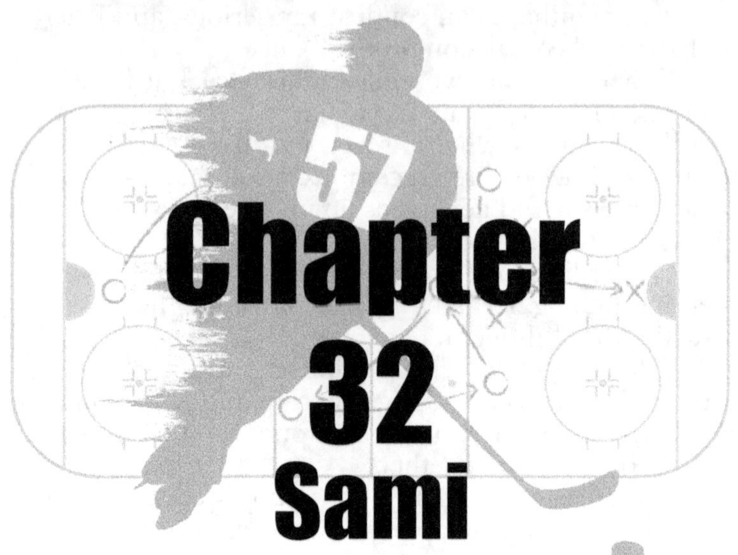

# Chapter 32
# Sami

Fuck it, I think to myself as I feel my back press the bedroom door open. Is this a smart move, or what I need to be doing now? Probably not, but I'll be damned if I'm going to stop it now. I'll deal with the aftermath later.

Kane's hands are everywhere at once, pulling restlessly at my clothing as we stumble across the floor. One roughened hand shoots up the back of my shirt and snaps at my bra clasp without missing a step, making me squeal when the garment releases.

"You always were too good at that," I mutter against his lips as he sets me down on the mattress, snagging the hem of my dress and pulling it over my head in one smooth move.

His cocky smirk is all I get as he pulls the straps down my arms, before pressing me down against the bedding.

"Didn't you hear you complaining," he retorts as he presses my hands to the pillows above my head, holding my wrists loosely in one large hand. "Keep your hands there, like a good girl."

I chew on my bottom lip but leave my hands there, watching as he stands back up, pulling his own shirt off before reaching for his belt, ripping it through the loops on his pants with such force it wraps around him and smacks against his leg.

I can't stop the squeal I make or the drawing up of my legs as the belt snaps. Even worse, he knows. He knows that beyond those visible reactions, I felt flutters and sparks everywhere. He's going to capitalize on that move in three, two…

He grabs the waistband of my panties in two strong handfuls, and slides them down my legs faster than I can move. With lightning reflexes he's on me, his warm body a comforting weight as his lips crash into mine again, his hips grinding, the friction of his fly sending sparks through me. Without thinking, I bring my hands down from where he told me to keep them, my fingers digging into his hair.

"Naughty girl," he groans, grabbing my hands and placing them back against the pillow. "I said keep your hands still."

"Sorry," I breathe, as he shifts down my body, pressing warm kisses on my fevered skin at my collarbone, between my breasts, and trailing toward my belly button. Jesus, the man was single minded.

Calloused palms pressed my thighs apart, leaving me helpless and exposed to his gaze. A thumb swipes against me, gathering the wetness on its tip.

"Look at you," he groans, slipping it just deeper into me, before pulling back out to circle my clit. "So fucking wet for me."

My back arches as he changes the pressure, the air rushing from my lungs. He's going to kill me at this rate, but I almost don't care.

"Just fuck me already, I can't…"

"Yes, you can. Give it to me."

With lightning fast speed, he lowers his head, replacing his thumb with his tongue before slipping two fingers inside. Lightning flashes behind my eyelids as I feel my muscles tense around him.

"That's my girl," he growls, sliding his fingers free and licking them clean, his eyes rolling back. With a quickness, he reached across to his night stand, grabbed a condom, and sheathed himself before settling between my legs. Pressing my thighs apart, he sat his hips forward, drawing himself through my slickness. "Are you ready?"

All I could manage was a quick nod before he shifted again, notching himself at my entrance, and thrust home. We groaned at the same time, eyes locked on each other as he rocks and grinds himself against me, withdraws, and then repeats the slow, torturous move again.

He's going to be the death of me. My legs wrap around him, trying desperately to pull him closer, faster, anything to control the speed.

"I don't think so, wife," he growls. "Patience." My eyes roll back in my head at the title. I should be offended, pissed that he's using it, but it does something to me. "Oh, you like that, do you?"

"Don't tease," I whisper, shifting restlessly underneath him.

"You like it when I call you 'wife,' when I claim you like this don't you?" A moan escapes my lips, and he grins ferally, pressing into me harder with a hissed breath between his teeth. "Are you mine?"

"Yes," I gasp on a moan, arching back into him.

"Say it," he commands.

"I…"

"Say you're mine." His large hand comes around my throat, the pressure, drawing my head back.

"I'm yours," I whisper.

"Louder. I'm not stopping until you scream my name."

"Oh god, Kane, I'm yours," I cry, moaning.

"Good girl, that's it," he croons, massaging his hand down to squeeze my breast lightly. "Give me one more."

My head shakes, I don't think I have it in me. His words don't stop, talking me through until with one last thrust I shatter around him. My vision darkens around the edges as I float through the last of my orgasm, feeling him pulse within me.

"Come here," he murmurs, wrapping a hand around the back of my neck, pulling me upright. His mouth closes on mine, a searing pressure as he glides his hands up and down my sweat-slicked back. "My wife," he says, dropping gentle kisses along my jawline.

"What are you– oh," I gasp, as he tugs on my earlobe with his teeth.

"I'm not done with you yet," he whispers, kissing the spot just under my ear that makes my eyes roll back.

"I never should have told you about that spot," I groan, trying to right my vision again.

"No, I need to find that spot more often," he counters, shifting me onto my back.

"I knew you were trouble," I choke out, his teeth closing lighting on my nipple.

"You never complained before." I look down into his mischievous grin as he slides down to press a kiss beside my belly button.

"Still not complaining," I sigh, as he continues his sweet torture. Yep, Definitely not complaining.

# Chapter 33
# Kane

I wake up and stretch with a groan, relishing in that feeling of my joints tensing and releasing in a series of pops, like bubble wrap. Being an older player sucks balls, but stretching has always felt oddly satisfying. Rolling over, I reach for Sami.

And reach. And again.

Stretch farther, and feel nothing but cool sheets under my fingertips.

Where the hell did she go?

I jump out of the bed and look around. Her things are gone. It's like she was never here to begin with. Her purse isn't even on the bar.

She left. She vanished into thin air and left me to wake up this morning all alone.

Growling, I grab my rumpled pants off of the floor, and take long strides to the front door. I'll be damned if she just up and leaves me again like this.

Pausing with my hand on the doorframe, my eyes roll in annoyance as I head back into my room, retrieving my shirt and my phone, then leave for good. I know exactly where she is, and I'm not giving her the chance to escape me.

Not like the last time.

"You're – you're Kane Blackwood," the valet

gasped trying to keep my keyfob from landing on the concrete. Should I have handed it off like I have manners? Sure. Do I care? No.

"Yeah, I am. I'll be right back," I say over my shoulder, not slowing my strides into the spacious lobby and into an elevator. Glaring at the nearby guests ensured I had a car all to myself. I really was in no position to be polite this morning.

My knuckles ached as I pounded against the wood.

"Kane?" Sami says, her voice muffled coming through the crack in the door.

"You left. Why?"

"One moment." She sighs as she closes the door, undoes the security bar, and opens the door wider for me. Waffles sit on a table, steam still rising from them. She had clearly come back and showered, damp tendrils hanging around her shoulders, leaving dark lines on the gray hoodie.

"It's not that serious, Kane. It's fine."

"What do you—I mean, why—how?"

I couldn't compute the words coming out of her mouth. Last night was just what? Nothing? I can't wrap my head around it.

"Kane. We said no strings. I'm a big girl, I can make my own waffles in the morning. Or, in this case, order them from room service." She waved her arm behind her, showing me a table with fruit, waffles and coffee.

"I know we said no strings, but I thought you would at least stick around."

She sighs, motioning to the bed so I would sit down. I collapse on the mattress, my elbows resting on my knees as I watch her sit down in the cushioned chair across from me, cross-legged, and pull the cup of coffee closer to her.

"Do you want some? I can order something different if you want?"

I shake my head, and motion for her to keep going. Guilt twists in my gut, I'm interrupting her breakfast with a heavy conversation that I don't even know if she wanted.

"I thought we could…I don't know, hang this

afternoon before your flight." The words feel weak on my tongue, not at all the confident man I usually present. I cringe a bit. I sound like me in high school when I was still scared to talk to girls.

"Kane, look at me," she says softly. I lift my head to make eye contact with her, watching her smile softly at me. "It's fine, okay? My flight is in a few hours anyway, there's not really enough time."

"You really like to downplay my skills."

I take a sip of my coffee again. "Your skills?"

He nods, taking a long pull from his water. "Finish your breakfast, Samantha. You're going to need the energy."

# Chapter 34
# Sami

I can absolutely move on like nothing happened this weekend.

I don't have beard burn from his stubble, or the beginnings of a hickey on my hipbone. I definitely don't have sore muscles, either. And I also didn't sleep on the plane because someone kept me up all night.

Nope. Didn't happen, can't prove it.

He called to make sure I went home okay, and then almost didn't let me off the line when I said I needed to unpack and get Gabby ready for school. It felt like…it felt like being back at the hockey house.

The feeling is bittersweet, because I had some of my best memories hanging with the guys at the house. It wasn't an official thing, it just happened to be that they were all able to room together in the same house. The fact that they were all hockey players and had the same schedules, that was just coincidence. Fate. Something.

Kane and I would spend hours at the dining room table, doing our homework together. He was so competitive, he needed to have the best grades, score better, skate faster than everyone. What started as just communal studying in the same area, eventually turned into collaboration. When it was too hard to focus on the work in the dining room, we would take turns studying in each others' rooms. Study buddies and friends turned to something so much more.

I really thought we were endgame goals then. Maybe I was young and dumb. I believed him when he said he would wait for me, that we would never be apart, that we would graduate together, he would go to the draft, and then we would get married.

How we would do it fresh out of college, most likely with him on a developmental contract at a smaller league, I would never know. Also, the absolute heart attack when our friends and family—especially Elliot— found out that this had been going on for a couple years under their noses? It was a recipe for disaster but we were committed to it. Or so I thought.

Silly dreams of a silly girl, I guess. I shake the thoughts loose, I don't have time for what might have been.

Holding Gabby again centers me. This is what matters, and what I have. I just need to get Kane on board, and move forward with life. Once we get this done, we can go our separate ways and I never have to worry about him again. I can't get attached, I have to stand my ground.

He's here for a good time, not for a long time. If I learned nothing else from our previous relationship, it is definitely this.

A knock at the door breaks me from my thoughts, and I open it to find a delivery driver with an envelope. I sign on the tablet, and take it back inside. I'm expecting to hear from Gabby's doctor, so I tear open the envelope excitedly.

Instead of documents, I'm greeted with pictures, photo upon photo of me and Kane on the last trip. Black and white shots of me taking Gabby to school, to the hospital. Even some photos of me at work. My heart races. Who took these? Where did they come from? Tucked inside is a small envelope, and opening it, I'm greeted by five words:

Stay Away From My Man.

Kane, what the hell have you gotten me into?

# Chapter 35
# Kane

I thought I was stronger than this.

Sitting at a bar, waiting on Vinny to show, and all I can think of is I want to be with Sami. Jesus, she has me so wrapped around her finger and the worst part is that I know how I got there.

I've always been there. I never stopped.

Who was I kidding? I fell in love with her years ago and I never fell out of love with her. I just left everything on hold. I threw most of the country between us and assumed that was a big enough wall to hide it.

It wasn't.

Seeing her again just destroyed every boundary and protection I had around my heart. I reverted right back into that lovesick kid, and the rest is history.

And I'm not even upset about it. Not even a little bit.

I haven't even met Gabby yet and I can already tell she's just like Sami. God, that woman. She shouldered all of this without me for so damned long. So much strength.

Fuck, I love her.

It's killing me to stay over here and not be with her, make a home with her, do everything we had talked about. But what do I have to offer her? A bachelor pad in Vegas with my questionable acquaintances? Seriously. I can't uproot them. I couldn't even consider asking that of her.

"Kane, what's up?" Vinny's booming voice breaks me out of my train of thought, and I turn to him.

"Vinny, I need you to do something for me. I know my contract is up and you've been trying to make deals to keep me here, but I want out. I want Rockville."

"You…you want to leave Vegas."

"Yeah, I want to set up in Rockville. Make it happen. I don't care what the costs."

"And…Rockville? Isn't that where…"

"Yeah, that's where Elliot and Sami are, I know."

"You know, Mikey is going to have some words about this. And Francesca."

"I really don't care about what she thinks, and Vinny, I'm done. I'm just tired. I've done my job. Let me go."

"It's not as easy as all that, buddy, and you know that."

"I don't care. He can let me go."

He sighs. "I'll see what I can do, but it's not going to be easy, I hope you know that."

"Just make it happen. You've managed to do everything else to keep us safe, I'm asking you this one time to do what I want."

"I'll ask around. What's the worst that happens, he kidnaps you and keeps you here?" He chuckles humorlessly, and I know he's right.

There has to be a way to do this. I won't mess this up again.

# Chapter 36
## Sami

Pulling in to the driveway after another appointment, listening to Gabby speak about the happenings at school earlier in the day, and I pause. There is a box on the porch. I don't remember ordering anything, but it wouldn't be the first time that Elliot and Ronni sent something.

"A box, mama! Can I open it?"

"Wait, baby, let me see who it's from first, okay?"

"Aw, okay." I drop a text to Ronni, and just on a lark, I send one to Kane too.

Me: Strange box on my doorstep…

Kane: Oh yeah? Maybe you should open it.

Me: Is it from you?

Kane: Maybe…

What the hell is he up to?

I take the box, open the door, and close it behind Gabby.

"I'll be back downstairs to make dinner, sweetie. Why don't you put away your school things and watch TV for a little bit, okay?"

"Okay, mama!" She scampers off, her energy level perking up.

As she disappears around the corner, I inspect the box. What could he have sent me?

I carefully cut open the tape, pulling back the flaps to see what is inside.

Eyeballs stare sightlessly up at me, in varying sizes. I suspect they were animal eyes, but oh my god, who sends this?

My fingers are numb and shaky as I pick up my phone. Somehow, I manage to dial Kane's number on the first try.

"Hey, beautiful. Did you like it?"

"What. The fuck. Did you send me?"

Silence hangs thick between us, and all I can hear is my pulse in my own ears.

"What do you mean? I sent you a copy of your favorite book! What did you get?"

I turn on the video call, and wait for his face to appear on the screen. He looks concerned, lines etched in his forehead.

"Show me."

I turn the camera around and show him the box, hearing him curse.

"Baby, that isn't mine. Where did that come from?"

I show him the label. The return address looks like a company of some sort.

"If you didn't send it—who did?"

"I have an idea. I'll take care of it, just," he sighs. "Trust me. I know I'm asking a lot, but trust me."

"Fine. Should I call the cops, though?"

"No! No cops. I'll take care of it."

"What the hell is this, Kane? What should I do?"

"Throw it out. Don't let Gabby see it. And for the love of God, please set your alarms."

With shaky hands, I close the box back up, and walk out the back door to place it directly into my trash bin. I don't know who or what he's dealing with, but this is making me nervous. With another glance around my yard, and a chill trickling down my spine, I head back into the house, locking the door behind me.

# Chapter 37
## Kane

Setting up a meeting with Francesca is either the best or worst decision I can make.

Vinny knows all of the details. I do trust him. I think. He's been in this with me since the beginning, and has always made sure we end up on the right side of Michael O'Connor.

I think Vinny is even disgusted by Francesca's actions. She's crossed a line. What if Gabby had opened that box? I shudder. I don't even know the kid but this is so far past acceptable. Who leaves this shit where a kid can find it?

Sitting at a table in Mikey's club, waiting for her to show, it takes everything I have to keep the rage from boiling over. Stay calm, stay cool. Talk it out. Deep breath in, deep breath out.

"Kane, baby, so nice to see you," she greets me, all smiles. I don't even get up from the table, I just look at her and motion to the seat across from me. She tilts her head in confusion. "You're not going to get my chair for me? Poor form. That's okay, I'll fix you."

"Sit down, please." My words are cool, direct, but neutral.

"Fine." She sets her designer purse on the table beside her plate, and takes a seat. Her eyes lock on mine, smile firmly in place. "I wondered when you would ever ask me on a date—"

"This isn't a date, Francesca."

"No? It's dinner, is it not?"

"Exactly. I asked to meet you because we need to have a conversation."

"All business, then. I see." Her face falls a bit before she slides that unaffected mask back into place. No wonder I didn't see this coming.

"We need to talk about Samantha."

"Who?"

"Don't play dumb, Francesca, it doesn't suit you. I know you know who I'm talking about."

She nods her head. "I don't have the slightest idea."

"Really? You didn't send eyeballs to her? Or pictures of us together? Who else would have?"

"Honestly, Kane, you act like I'm some common thug in my Uncle's company. I don't need to do anything barbaric like that." She takes a sip of the wine in front of her. "She's not worth spending that much time on, if we're being serious. I mean, she lives on the other side of the country and hasn't given you the time of day in years. She's an annoyance, and once you get over that, you'll come back to me."

What is she even talking about?

"Francesca, I've tried to tell you. There is no 'us,' and there never will be. I'm sorry if you picked up signals like that, but I'm not interested. You're a great person, you just aren't for me."

I watch her closely, her face darkening as she looks at me. "Kane. You've left me no choice. Forget about her, or else."

"Or else what, Francesca? Look, I did your uncle a favor and escorted you to a few parties. I did it out of respect for him. But this needs to stop. Now."

"Don't make this harder than it has to be, Kane. Forget about the girl."

"It doesn't have to be like this," I say to her. "I don't understand why you're fighting so hard for us to have a relationship that I don't want."

"I always get what I want, and the sooner you

figure this out, the sooner we can put this nastiness behind us."

"So you're going to do what? Blackmail me into dating you? That's the route you want to go with this?"

She lifts a shoulder, as if the question is as small as if she'd prefer the fish or chicken. "So what if I do? You'll deal with it. You have every time my uncle has asked you to work for him. You'll grow to accept it."

# Chapter 38
# Sami

The results came today. He's a match.

I knew in my gut that this would be the case, but to see it, in black and white, is another thing altogether. It can't be taken back now, we can't stuff it back into Pandora's Box, it's official.

I know he received the same letter as well, but now we need to make plans. He won't be able to do the draw until after the season, in just a few weeks. It will be fine. We'll get there.

Elliot is coming over in a little bit so I can tell him. He still doesn't know names, and that's just fine. It's on a "need to know" basis and it doesn't matter where it's coming from.

"Hey, Samsquatch, you here?" Elliot comes through my kitchen, helping himself to my fridge and stepping over the coffee table to flop onto my couch.

"Comfy there, big guy?" I ask with a laugh.

"Yeah, I think I am. How have you been? I never see you anymore."

"I know, our schedules have been weird, haven't they? We need to do dinner again. Soon."

"Ronni wanted me to invite you over Friday if you're free."

"I should be. But I have something I need to tell

you first."

"Hit me. Is it good? Bad? You kind of had me nervous on the phone."

"It's…it's good. It's a definite match, and we're planning on the marrow draw soon. It's happening, El. It's really happening!"

"That's great! How does Gabby feel, does she know?"

"She knows. She's nervous but excited at the same time."

"Great news! Any idea when?"

"We're hoping to hold off until after the season ends. It would just be easier. And that gives us time to build up her immune system beforehand, and for you and Ronni to be free too. You wouldn't focus during the playoffs otherwise."

"Good, good." He nods his head. "Yeah, you have a point. So, is he a hockey player too? I know you said his name doesn't matter, but he's doing something kind of major here, sis."

"I know, I'm just," I bite my lip as I think about it. "I think it would be better if you just didn't know. And he's been fine with being anonymous."

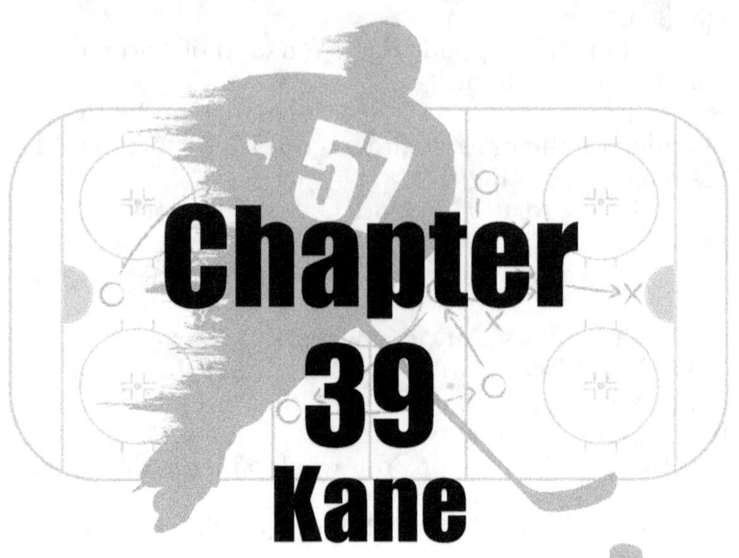

# Chapter 39
## Kane

Who knew conversations with my ex would be so infuriating?

Once again I stare at the screen of my phone, the string of unanswered texts in front of me. I swear she does this on purpose sometimes. All I want – or need, really – is for her to answer her damned texts so we can set up a meeting. Vinny and Braxton are certain that we need to establish paperwork, boundaries, before we enter into this adventure. I have zero problem going into a clinic and giving them whatever it is they need. I already researched my side, it's non-invasive and I can do it whenever the hell I want. Their concern is that this would open the door for anything on Sami's end. First it's some cells, then it's a bill here or there, then I'll be on the hook for back support with interest. The joke's on them, though, because I've already calculated the rate I should've paid and have it in an account already, with Sami's name on it.

The biggest part, the scariest part of all of this, is that I want out of Vegas. I want to be there. I can't understand the guilt I feel for not being present in the moment, leaving her alone with all of this. If I'm honest, I'm guilty about abandoning her and leaving a decent friend to deal with the aftermath. Does Elliot piss me off? To no end, yes. But he still didn't ask for this either.

"Answer your fucking phone, Samantha," I growl at my phone, as her chipper voicemail message plays for me again.

Fine. So be it.

Me: I need to coordinate for our legal teams to talk. Can you make that happen?

Dots appear on the bottom of my screen, then stop. They reappear, then go away again.

Sami: I'll let you know.

"Fucking finally," I sigh, laying my head back on my shoulders, closing my eyes in relief.

I swear, she has always made me work harder, longer, and faster for everything in life. She wouldn't let me skate by on just being a hotshot hockey player. No, I had to actually do my work. And barely meeting standards wasn't enough. I had to strive to be the best, to prove to her I could do it.

Maybe she's why I play the way I do. Maybe it was always there, and she just unlocked it. All I know is that I haven't been able to stop trying to do better, be better, than everyone around me for the longest time.

My phone rings, and I groan as I look at the screen. Vinny's name is on the screen, and I know if I don't answer it, he's going to just call right back. I swipe to answer, tilt back in my chair, and settle in for a long conversation.

"What do you have for me, Vinny?"

"I think I have the answer to your prayers, man. Are you ready for this?"

I lean back forward, resting my elbows on the desk and focus.

"What did you find out?"

"The Ice Wolves will take you on. You're going to be taking a little bit of a pay cut–"

"Done."

# Chapter 40
## Sami

My gut churns again as I look down at yet another text from Kane. This time he's asking — kudos for using his manners, I guess — for a meeting between his legal team and mine. As if I have a legal team. I don't keep lawyers on retainer, I'm not a hotshot hockey player! Sure, Elliot would probably let me borrow the lawyer in charge of his work, but I already depend on Elliot for so much. He won't leave me to fend for myself, always ready to swoop in and save the day. Trevor already locked down his lawyer friend but won't tell me how much it costs to use her. What I end up making is tied up between household expenses and hospital bills, so it isn't like I have the extra money laying around to pick my own, either.

I have to talk this out with someone and figure out how to get out of this mess, but I can't talk to anyone around me who is overloaded with testosterone and a caveman ideal to protect his womenfolk, even if it is with the best intentions. No, I know who I need to talk to, she's made a career out of this.

I need to talk to Ronni. Clearly. I mean, if she could fix Elliot's personal life before it imploded on his professional life, I'm sure she could help me with this one. Which is why I find myself standing outside of the doorway with the black plastic sign declaring it the office of one Veronica Snow, soon to be Veronica Snow-Moxley.

"Hey Ronni." I peek my head inside the open doorway in time to catch her lightly rolling back and forth in her white leather office chair, watching the light dance off of the diamond ring on her left finger with a soft smile on her face.

She comes to with a start, straightening in her chair and giving the appearance that she wasn't just daydreaming in the middle of business hours.

"Hey Sami, good to see you! I don't think I've seen you since you came back from Vegas!"

Ouch, there it was. The elephant in the room. "Yeah, about that," I pause looking out in the hallway. "Do you have some time, I need to talk to you and this may not be fast. Or easy. I just don't know who else to talk to."

"Absolutely, come on in! Please, sit!" She comes around her desk to a pair of armchairs flanking a squat coffee table. "Would you like some water? Coffee? My poor assistant has no idea what to do for me, she'd appreciate the work," she laughs, and I can only imagine how it is. She always worked on everything by herself, or at most with her best friend and teammate Jessica. Now that they worked separately, she was apparently still struggling to delegate her workload.

"I'm good, thanks, though." We sit down, and I pick at my nails, contemplating. "I may have made a mistake going to Vegas, and I don't know how to get out of it now."

"Oh no, are you okay? What happened?"

"Yeah, I think so. If I tell you something, can you not tell Elliot yet? I'm not sure how he's going to take this."

"That sounds scary."

"It could be. There's unofficial rules in hockey, Ronni. Don't stand on the team logo in the locker room. Don't let your Jersey hit the floor. But there's one that's bigger than that."

"What is it?"

"Your teammates' sisters are off limits. Don't

touch."

"Sami, are you saying…"

"I know who Gabby's father is. El knows him too. They played together for years."

"Oh no. Is he on this team now?"

"No, this was in college. However, he is in the league, just on another team."

"You'll need to tell him at some point, Sami, that's big. Does her father know?"

"That's why I went on that trip a few weeks ago. I went to talk to him in person to see if he would test for compatibility for Gabby's marrow."

"Did he agree to it?"

"He didn't get back to me right away about if he would, but I did get a call from her doctor today. He tested and it matched, both for paternity and compatibility. I haven't answered his text messages yet about getting lawyers together or talking. At all."

"Oh, Sami, you need to talk to him. Do you need a lawyer? I've talked to a few through the Foundation events, I can get their information for you."

"That would be awesome, it's on my list but I just don't know where to start. I mean, this is massive. Plus, Elliot is going to be pissed, I'm sure. They used to be best friends, but I don't think they've talked since they were drafted."

Ronni looks at me chewing thoughtfully on her bottom lip. "I have a question, and you don't have to answer it if you don't feel comfortable with it. But, who is her father?"

I know I can trust her. So after taking a breath I whisper, "Blackwood."

"Who?"

"Kane Blackwood. He's her father."

"What. The Actual. Fuck." We both jump and turn toward the door where Elliot is blocking the doorway.

I clear my throat, hoping to sound unbothered. "El, hi, I didn't know you'd be —"

"Don't 'El' me, what the hell do you mean that Kane is Gabby's father? You two never dated! Did he take advantage of you? I knew I should've broken his nose earlier than I did," he growled, stepping into the room.

"And this is why you never told him, right?" Ronni's stage whisper carried to me as we both froze, not taking our eyes off of Elliot.

"Yup," I answered softly, as I started to get up off of the seat. "El, I'm serious. I am taking care of it, you don't need to go all caveman about it. We made choices, as adults, and it was my choice not to say who her father was. Is. Whichever."

"You were a freshman, Samantha! You barely turned 18 before– ! Fuck!" His roared expletives had to have been heard the entire length of the hallway and I cringed at the volume.

Well, the cat is definitely out of the bag now.

# Chapter 41
## Kane

So, This is home now.

Staring up at the gleaming entryway of Theodore J Price Arena, the giant glass facade plastered with the Ice Wolves logo and massive portraits of Elliot Moxley, Val Bishop, and the rest of their team — my team, I correct — I feel my stomach turn. It's like the first day in a new school, in a way. Nervous energy thrummed through me.

It wasn't easy, but it needed to be done. Over the last few weeks, I initiated a trade to put me here. I needed to be here to attempt to salvage a relationship with my daughter. A daughter who didn't even know I existed and, as the tests revealed, needed me. Sami still hadn't answered any of my calls this week. I know she received the documents from Braxton last week, only because the courier checked her ID and I recognized the signature on the receipt. Still, though, she hadn't said a word to me since that phone call before she left Vegas.

I'm set to meet with the PR team so they can make the announcement about the trade official. My boys in Vegas all knew, naturally. They took me out one last time before I coordinated for the movers to take everything I owned and move it across the country.

Now, I'm home. On the East Coast for the first time in damn near a decade for more than a few days at a time. I walk through the doors, looking around at the vast entry way, my steps echoing in the open space.

"Toto, we definitely aren't in Kansas anymore," I murmur. I'm determined to keep a positive outlook on this thing. I know I asked for it, but I'm still not super excited about it. But responsibilities are responsibilities, plus it would look better if I made an attempt to forge a relationship instead of just throwing money at the situation. As if that would fix a damn thing.

Voices are carrying to me, and I look toward the mezzanine above me. The murmur of an argument got louder and then I could make out the words.

"I'm going to cut his pencil dick off with my damn skate! He fucking touched you, Sami!" Shit. That's Elliot. His yelling could always be heard clearly over the chaos of a game, I could recognize that voice anywhere.

"El, be reasonable. You can't physically hurt —" Is that Sami?

"The hell I can't! He touched you and left you knocked up! What kind of asshole does that?"

"Kind of aware of that, I was there when it happened after all!" Yep, that was definitely Sami. A feminine gasp broke between the brash words.

"Sami, that's not helping, love. El, babe, be reasonable—"

"I am being reasonable!" His bellow echoed off the open space. "There is a code of conduct and he didn't follow it!"

"What's next, a pistol duel at dawn? El, I went and talked to him already —"

"You're going to talk to my lawyer. He owes you for this bullshit."

"I'm a grown ass adult, Elliot, will you let me take care of this like one?"

They were standing at the top of the stairs, Sami glaring up at Elliot, her hands balled up at her sides. Elliot is red faced and staring down at her, not giving up an inch. Between them, a shorter curvy woman kept her eye on both of them, her hands held up, ready to separate them if needed, like an MMA ref. That must be Veronica Snow.

With a growl, Elliot stomps down the stairs, still oblivious to my presence. Probably a good thing, because I have a feeling he would have jumped from the landing to attack me.

"El, seriously, you're blowing this out of proportion. Just come back here——"

"No! He knew better. He knew you were off-limits, and now I get to break his nose for it. Again."

"You're such a Neanderthal sometimes! Will you chill the hell out so we can talk?"

Oh, this was going to suck, but I had nowhere to go now. If I go back out the door now, he'll chase me down in the street. If I tried to go anywhere else, he'd see me move. Looks like it's gloves down, tarps off. I clear my throat loudly, interrupting their arguing. Three sets of eyes lock on me from above; Elliot's narrow in anger, Veronica's wide in surprise, and Sami's panicked gaze.

"Hello, wife."

# Chapter 42
## Sami

Kane Blackwood stared up at us from the entryway, hands in his jeans pockets and his eyes locked defiantly on me. God only knew how much he heard from there, but from his stance, he had heard enough. While his general posture looked calm and relaxed, I could see that tick in his jaw from the balcony railing. I had watched him in play enough to know that was the look he had in his eye before he threw down gloves and unleashed on an opponent, penalty minutes be damned. I could only imagine who he planned to throw down with now.

"What the hell does he mean? Wife? Are you — did you — what the fuck, Sami?" Elliot's glare shot from me, to Kane, back to me. A red flush climbed his neck and The tennis-match gaze would have been entertaining in any other scenario.

"I told you I'd file an annulment," I countered back at Kane. "What are you doing here?"

"Pretty sure we're past the point of annulment, babe. We have DNA involved now."

"You fucking prick, I'm gonna—" Elliot started to unleash a verbal assault on him while launching toward the stairs. Ronni tried to pull him backward, her heels clicking against the cement floor as she tried to gain leverage.

"Elliot, stop," Ronni begged, her small hands hooked around his elbow, trying to drag him back from the stairs.

It was all I could do to keep the hysterical laughter inside of me. What kind of fever dream is this? Seriously?

"To hell with this," I mutter, shaking my head. Stepping up the stairs, I shoved Elliot off-balance enough that he moved out of the way and started walking down the stairs. "What do you want, Kane? We can make this all disappear and you can go back home to Vegas. I don't know why you came all the way over here to find me."

"Funny story," he says, smirking as I step down on even footing with him. "Home is now at the Arlington Towers."

I feel my heart plummet as I stare at him. That's where Elliot lives. "You're kidding."

"Nope. I signed papers yesterday. I'm supposed to be meeting with coach today. Looks like your brother and I will be playing together again."

"The fuck you are! We'll see how long you stick around!" Elliot's barb echoed around us, but I didn't look away from Kane.

"You can undo all of this and go back to Vegas. I definitely don't want or need you here." He smirked. That cocky motherfu-

"Pretty sure you need me here a little bit. Or did you not need my marrow?"

"You don't have to be here to help, though."

"True, but this works for both of us." His gaze shoots past me to where I can hear Elliot and Ronni in a hushed argument at the top of the stairs. "Any chance Mom and Dad up there will let you out after curfew? We need to talk but I'm supposed to be in a meeting with ownership soon."

"I'm a grown adult, Kane, I make my own schedule. But yes, we do need to talk, you're right. We need to get to the bottom of this."

"I'll call you when I'm out. I need to meet up with the team soon, but we seriously need to talk this out.

You'll answer this time?"

I cringe, thinking of all the missed calls on my phone. "Yeah, I'll answer."

"I'll hold you to it. Later, babe." I know I roll my eyes at him, and he chuckles, winking at me. With another look over my shoulder, he walks off toward the elevator for the head offices. I stand, frozen, watching him go, and contemplate how I'm going to fix this.

I take a deep breath and turn around to where Elliot and Ronni are still lingering at the top of the stairs, and she is clearly telling him to keep out of it for the moment.

# Chapter 43
# Kane

"Welcome to Rockville, Blackwood." Commissioner Andrews stands, reaching out a large hand to me for a firm handshake. The lighting over the boardroom table glints off the gems in the massive ring resting between his knuckles; a ring for winning the Cup back when he played. I have to admit, playing for a team owned by a former player doesn't feel bad at all.

"Thank you, sir, I'm excited to be here." I look over at the mural of the ice, the giant snarling wolf head logo at center ice. As many times as I've played here, I've never looked at it from this angle before. The pristine white, broken up by the bright blue and red circles and lines, the clean image makes me feel more at home for the first time in days.

"I remember watching the tapes of you and Moxley working together for the Buckeyes. You two were a force to be reckoned with. Have to admit, I'm hoping to put you two back on a line together for the rest of the season, don't know if anyone will see it coming."

I cringe inwardly a little bit. A lot has changed since then, and I'm pretty sure that the teamwork we experienced then will have a hard time coming back together. We're going to ignore the fact that Moxley took a 2-game suspension for busting my nose last year, I guess.

"We're a little rusty on that part, I think, but I'm open to anything that will get us another Cup, sir."

"That's what I'm talking about! Coach should be up here in just a moment, and our PR team. I'm sure they're going to want to get the social media updated with our branding."

"Speaking of branding is music to my ears," a woman's voice called from the open doorway. "Hi, I'm Jessica, I'm going to be your main point of contact for everything." She holds out a small, delicate hand with teal nail polish, and I take it in what I hope is a gentle handshake. "We'll coordinate schedules and get your photo shoot and media packet done before the next game."

"I'm looking forward to it. My personal assistant has been trying to replace all of my social media but I know it's driving him crazy to not have updated team photos."

She drops into a leather chair and begins pulling out a laptop and notebooks, setting up for our meeting. I hear men talking in the hallway, and before long the doorway is filled with the large frames of Coach and Val Bishop, one of the alternates.

"Coach, Val, come on in." Commissioner Andrews greets them individually with a sharp handshake, before introducing me to both. Coach's handshake is firm and quick, but Val practically crushes my hand in his.

"Blackwood," he growls, tightening his grip one more time before trying to step away.

"Bishop," I reply, giving a firmer grip in return. He doesn't scare me. I don't care if he is Moxley's new best friend.

"Let's sit down and get schedules figured out here, so Blackwood comes up to speed quickly. We're running out of time before the All-Star break ends."

I sit to the left of the commissioner, coach and Val across from me, and Jess is to my left. Val's eyes bounce between me and Jess, and she doesn't even look up at him.

Coach starts talking about practice schedules and I shift my focus to him, typing into my calendar app on the required dates and times. I sense movement around my foot and glance over toward Val and Jess, who are both locked in a stare down now. If I'm not mistaken Val's foot is…shifting to our side of the table? I shift my eyes back to Coach and the conversation he's still having with the commissioner, but yes, pretty sure that was Val Bishop's pant leg. What the hell is he doing?

Jess, coughs slightly and I catch her shifting out of the corner of my eye. I start to throw more reminder texts to my PA, and feel that movement— again. I shoot a look at Val, who is doing his damnedest to look nonchalant, but clearly he's searching out Jess and she isn't having it. Again, his shoe bumps against mine.

"Hey, sweetheart, you really should take me out to dinner first," I murmur, winking at the giant goalie across from me. He scowls, a muttered "whatever" and we all go back to listening to Coach. Moments later, it happens again, just as Jess starts talking to me about the photography schedule. "What the hell?" I whisper under my breath.

"Excuse me?" She stops everything to look squarely at me.

I gape at her. "I'm sorry, it's just—"

"OW! Sonofa—" Bishop curses, sliding his chair back to rub on his shin.

She never broke eye contact with me, and I'm pretty sure she just kicked the shit out of our top goalie. I pick up my water bottle, attempting to hide my grin behind the act of drinking.

"My apologies for your teammate, Mr. Blackwood."

"No problem. So, you were saying, full moon shoot? When?"

"Looks like in two weeks there's a full moon during a home game stretch, so if we can catch a night then, it would be great."

"Sounds good. I'm wide open." I lean over to swap numbers with her and I could feel Bishop's eyes boring into me. "Thanks, Jess, I appreciate it. But I think your boyfriend over there is about to punch me."

"He's not my boyfriend," she bites out, glaring at him across the table.

"Coulda fooled me." I notice Coach and the Commissioner starting to pay attention to us, and redirect my attention. "So, what do we have going on next? I have my PA on speed dial if I need something."

"The most important thing I need out of you," Coach starts, "is to keep your nose clean. Out of the news. I know Vegas has a relaxed set of rules for you boys, but we try to stay clean over here."

"Not a problem, sir. I'll be on my best behavior."

"About that," Jess interjects. "Any surprises I need to know about in advance? Explicit photos, secret love child, baby mama drama, anything that will put you in a bad light?"

Ouch.

"No, I'm good." I'll be damned if I'm going to tell her what's going on. I just got here, after all.

"It makes my job easier if I'm not blindsided, Blackwood. And they're reluctant to keep trouble on the team."

"I'll let you know if something comes up." I smile and wait for her to relax. She's not falling for it, but she makes a face and continues jotting down notes.

We settle back into regular conversation, but I can't focus. All I can think about is fixing things fast with Sami before things go wrong here and I find myself without a team.

# Chapter 44
## Sami

What. A. Disaster.

I escaped from the potential fist fight between Kane and Elliot and ran to The Den for coffee. That makes everything better, I'm sure of it. Staring into the foam, I try to figure out how the hell I got into this predicament.

Why is he moving here? Why didn't he take the contract extension in Vegas? I don't understand any of this.

Trevor is supposed to be coming in to meet me, and I am dying to tell him everything that has gone down today. There must be cameras somewhere, because I feel like I'm on one of those prank shows. Where else would this perfect storm happen?

"Sami, babe, what's up?" Trevor calls to me as he approaches my table.

"Trev, you would not believe the day I've had." Hopping down from the stool I've been on, I give him a hug.

"Tell me all about it."

"You remember how I came home and said Kane and I had made a mistake, right?"

"Yeah, and you've gone to visit him twice to do a favor for him. All tit-for-tat."

"Okay, so he was supposed to stay in Vegas. Not come here. He's here."

"What do you mean, 'he's here,' Sami?"

"He signed a contract with the Ice Wolves. He lives here now."

"No way," Trevor said, cackling. "That is so wild! Does Elliot know?"

I couldn't even say the word, I just bobbed my head up and down.

"Oh shit, he hates it doesn't he? Tell me everything. I want to know every delicious detail."

"They almost got into a fistfight at the arena. I'm pretty sure Elliot was down to break his nose again."

"Of course he did, your brother is massive and super protective of you. He spent months grilling me before he realized I didn't see you that way."

"I know, and some things just don't die with him. Apparently the grudge with Kane is going to last forever."

Trevor sips at his coffee, his brow crinkled in that way when he's deep in thought.

"So what is the plan?"

"Apparently Kane wants us to stay together, because he thinks I'm 'in danger' or something," I reply, rolling my eyes as I wave air quotes. "It's ridiculous. We don't need to live together to do any of this and I can't understand why he wants me to.

"I have an idea why, but you may not want to hear it."

My gaze narrows as I look at him, sitting primly and looking back at me over his cup, his posture relaxed, long legs crossed. He would wait me out until I asked what he thought.

# Chapter 45
## Kane

I did it. I've escaped Vegas, Francesca, and everything that held for me. I used to think Vegas was what I needed, or wanted in life. A huge house, expensive things, massive bank accounts, and adoring fans made me feel important, but in the end? None of it matters.

Wandering around my empty penthouse, the one I told Sami they needed to move into, my heart clenches. What the hell do I have to offer her? A big screen TV and boxes of bachelor shit? I need to make this place a home. We may not be here forever, but it still needs to be comfortable. How is Gabby going to be comfortable here? There is nothing I have that would be kid appropriate.

With a sigh, I walk over to the kitchen island, contemplating the decorators that Jess and Ronni recommended. Maybe they can soften up the house. God knows I don't know what I'm doing. If I do this, they might hate it. I don't care what color the walls are, or what the couch looks like. But maybe they do.

All I know for sure is the freedom I feel knowing that Francesca does not know where I am, that we have security in the building, and that I will have my wife and child in the house in a few days is making me breathe easier.

Fighting for # 57

Why I invited Sami into my house full of boxes is beyond me. I should have looked up a restaurant for her. This isn't the way to make her feel welcome, but I also didn't want to have these conversations in public. I'm not an excellent cook, usually having someone around to do it for me, but I managed to pull something edible together after setting up my kitchen.

Setting the table calms my nerves a bit, and before I know it, the doorbell rings. Sweaty palms smooth the wrinkles in my shirt and slacks.

"Well, it's too late to back out now, Blackwood," I mutter to myself before I open the door.

# Chapter 46
# Sami

This could go so much worse, I think to myself as I ride the elevator up to Kane's new place. Elliot said he could get him removed from the building because clearly, he's still harboring some feelings about the whole ordeal. I'm just resigned to it at the moment. I'll go, we'll talk, I'll get paperwork straight so we can quietly make this all go away. I'm sure of it.

I tap lightly on his door, finding it slightly ironic that his apartment sits in the same area of the hall as Elliot's, just a floor below him. Kane throws the door wide, a white dish towel slung over the black button down that he wore earlier today at the arena.

"Hey, I'm glad you could make it," he says, motioning me inside. "Dinner should only be a few more minutes, but I can get you some wine in the meantime."

"Actually, water would be great. It might be better if we kept sober heads this time around."

He ducks his head, his ears going red. "Yeah, I didn't think of that. I'll get you set."

I look around his living space, noticing how it still looks very much like Elliot's, perhaps without him knowing. I definitely won't say anything like that, the last thing I need is for them to get in a pissing match about sharing interior decorators.

"Can I help with dinner?" I ask as I set my purse down on an end table by the couch, before following him around to the kitchen island.

"If you want to pull out the caesar salad, that would be great, thanks." He's bent over, pulling something out of the oven. I bite my bottom lip as I watch his muscles bunch under his shirt and the way his pants shift…focus, Sami, I tell myself as I turn away quickly and open the refrigerator door.

I walk the salad bowl over to the broad table, placing it between the two place settings he had arranged. My eyebrows raise as I notice the details; linen napkins, more than one fork.

"Wow, Kane, real silverware and linen napkins? I'm impressed. I thought you would still be living out of boxes and we'd be eating takeout sitting in the living room."

"Ouch, you wound me. I do have some manners, Sami," he jibes, bringing over a platter with salmon and roast vegetables on it. "I remember you couldn't get enough of this back in the day, so…," he trails off, shrugging as he sets it down beside the salad and motions for me to sit. "Go ahead and dig in." He fills two glasses with ice water before coming back to the table, placing one by me and then one by his plate before sitting down himself.

"So, we have some things to talk about," I start, as I carefully lift a piece of the salmon to my plate.

"Yeah, I have some thoughts on the matter, if you're open to them," he responds, scooping some of the salad onto his plate across from me. "I had an enlightening experience with the team's PR, Jess seems to have very firm ideas on no surprises."

I giggle, as I remember the runaround that she experienced with Elliot. "Yeah, thank my brother for that one. He made Jess and Ronni earn their paychecks and almost got traded because of it."

"She did seem to be very specific about inappropriate photos," he replies, and we smile at each other. "She also mentioned that she didn't want any surprise paternity suits, marriages, or Vegas shenanigans coming out of the woodwork, and I can't help but wonder if she knows something."

I set my fork down on my plate. "I haven't told anyone, Kane. I only just told Ronni this afternoon while you were heading to the meeting with Jess. They may work fast, but they're not that fast."

"I didn't mean to make it sound like you told, but she did seem to be aware that it would be a PR nightmare she wanted to get ahead of. And I agree with her. To a point."

"So, what do you want to do about it? Especially now that Elliot and Ronni are in the know?"

"My thought," he says, pausing to drop a spoon of roasted vegetables on his plate, "is to not make any rash legal decisions. I think we should stay married."

I struggle to keep my sip of water in my mouth. "Excuse me? I know you didn't just say what I think you said."

"Just, hear me out for a minute, okay?" He takes a deep breath. "Let's say we keep things the way they are. We have a blood test establishing paternity, we now have documentation showing we're basically a nuclear family on paper. She gets her health care through me, we play happy family for a bit, the press eats it up, and no one is the wiser. Right?

"Except for the fact that you aren't on her birth certificate and that we haven't lived together, ever, and we've only been married for three weeks."

"I know, I know. So, we say the timing just was never right."

"In seven years we never had time to be in the same city at the same time. Sure. they're totally going to buy that," I scoff.

"We'll say you sprung it on me after watching Elliot and Ronni reconcile, and sure, we did the Vegas marriage thing, but no one needs to know the details except us."

"This is going to be a disaster," I mutter. "Seriously, Blackwood, how do you expect this to work? Do you expect me to uproot Gabby from everything she knows and move her into this," I wave a hand around at his spacious, empty penthouse. "And, how long do you expect this to go on? Do we go back our separate ways at the end of the season, or when there's a new **PR** spin for you to follow?"

He stares at me, wide eyed. "We can play it by ear, there's no need to put an absolute deadline on it. We'll just play along until it's just not cool anymore. You guys can come and stay here, and it's fine. Keep the other place, we'll just try to make this look like our home."

"You're going to need a lot of work." I could hear my words echo off the empty walls.

"Do what you want with the place. I mean, I most likely won't be here that often, anyway, between practices and away games."

"You're serious about this." The words slip out as I just stare at him.

His shrug was a little tentative. "I can't mess this up, Samantha. Vegas put up with a lot of shit, but this is a different thing altogether. I need to be on the good side of the administration. And honestly, it's time for me to quit dicking around and be mature. Make solid life choices. Things like that. I'm not a rookie anymore."

"You're not that old, Kane, you still have a lot of seasons ahead of you."

"I'm one puck drop away from a career ending injury, you know that. And maybe this has been an eye opening experience for me."

Staring at him, the silence heavy around us, I take in what he's saying.

"Kane," I start slowly, "what the fuck is wrong with you?"

# Chapter 47
## Kane

Fucking hell. She was always way too good at that.

My heart pounded as I let her words hang in the air unanswered. I'm sure I could trust her with this but I haven't told anyone outside of my personal trainer for a reason. The last thing I need is time riding the bench with an injury before I ever get settled on the new team.

"You can't tell anyone. Ever."

"Okay?" She draws out the word like a question, and then stares at me expectantly.

"I jacked up my knee." The words come out fast and muddled, even to my own ear.

"Say that again? Because it kind of sounded like you said you jacked up your knee, and I get the idea you haven't told anyone. Have you even had it looked at? X-rays, anything? Even if it's outside of the team facilities? Jesus, what's wrong with you?"

"Wow, that's intense, Sami." I run my fingers through my hair. "I'd almost think you cared."

"Don't be ridiculous, of course I care. You grew up with Elliot, and I don't actively want to see you hurt." She frowns at me, "Do you really think I would wish ill will on you because of our past?"

"Not exactly, but I may have earned it." I drop my head toward the table, rolling the edge of the napkin between my fingers, unable to control my nerves. "I would never have left you in that position had I known."

"I know. And maybe it was just my stubborn pride keeping me from telling you before now, but we kind of settled into our routines and it was just…easier." She's absolutely right. And she's telling the truth, which somehow soothes the ache that I've had in my heart for the last month.

"I really think that we can make this work, and everything will be fine. Can we at least try it until the end of the season? We can work the paperwork after the season ends and go our separate ways during the summer."

"I'm probably going to regret this, but okay. It's only until the end of the season. That's enough time for you to settle, get Gabby the treatment cycles, and then put off the paperwork stress for when you don't have the practice and game schedule interfering." She smooths her hands over her jeans  before holding out her hand to me. "It's a deal."

As I shake her hand, I can only hope that we're right.

# Chapter 48
## Sami

Fine. We'll do this. We'll pretend we're a little happy family.

My temple pounds and I feel the beginning of a stress headache behind my eyeball as I sit in the conference room with Elliot, Kane, and Ronni. Ronni is clearly trying to tell Elliot to stop staring at Kane, who dropped into the chair beside me and has been an antagonizing little shit the whole time.

"Wouldn't it just be easier to annul this thing? You do your thing, and I do mine?" I whisper at him.

"No, because I want to make sure you're safe."

"And how are you going to keep me safe if you're on the road?"

"We're moving into Elliot's building. You're coming with me. They have security. Your house doesn't."

"And Gabby? What about her? She doesn't know you enough for this."

"We'll get her accustomed to this and it will be fine. But I want you in my house. I want to keep you safe."

"And when you have to go on road trips? What then?"

"I'll drag you both with me if I need to. I'm not

leaving you alone."

"I still don't get why you have to live together," Elliot grumbles. "It's completely unnecessary and disrupts Gabby's routines. Even I know better than that. And I'm not even her dad."

Kane's jaw clenches at the jab, and I cringe a little inside. It's a low blow, even from my overprotective brother.

"If you want to know," Kane grits out between his teeth. "I have suspicions someone is trying to get to Sami because of me."

"And you thought coming into town and living with her was the smart move? Seriously, Blackwood? You just put out the bat signal to wherever she is. And my niece! What the ever loving fuck?"

"I feel better being in the house to protect her."

"And what about practice, and road games, and press, or weight training. You know, the things you have to do to get paid?" Kane reiterates everything I've been thinking and saying for days. "You can't be up her ass 24/7, you have a job to do."

"Elliot," Ronni says on a gasp, "that's not helping!"

"What? It's dumb and reckless, and I haven't helped her out so he can swoop in and save the day like some knockoff Superman. Fuck that."

"Elliot," I start, pinching the bridge of my nose. "It's fine. I know it's not ideal, but maybe there's some positives to it?"

"Like what?"

Kane's voice cuts in before I can say anything. "How about security for one thing. Moving her into the Tower means security at the door. You live there, tell me how safe you feel there."

Elliot glares at him for a moment. "Most of the team lives there, asshat. They have round the clock security and key card entry only on the upper floors and garage."

"So it's safer than having her in some townhouse across town, right?"

Elliot huffs a sigh. "Yes."

"Why you didn't move her in here earlier I'll never

understand," Kane snipes at Elliot, and I watch as Elliot starts to stand. Holding a hand out across the table in front of Kane, as if that would hold him back, I stare daggers into both men. Screw them and their pseudo-caveman posturing bullshit.

"I didn't want to live in the Tower with him, I wanted a regular neighborhood for Gabby. That was my choice. Not his. So walk that one back."

Kane seems to shift backward in the seat a little, crossing his arms across his chest.

"Either way, Sami, I would feel safer if you were there. Please." Kane's words were soft, but I could hear the conviction in his words. He was making good on his promise to keep us safe.

"Okay, fine. When are we moving?"

# Chapter 49
## Kane

Who knew that having a child in your house could be so wild.

Half of my kitchen is filled with snacks and treats shaped like cartoon characters, instead of the protein powder, peanut butter, and smoothie ingredients that I used to live off of. I didn't even think cereal came by those colors naturally, but there they were. Marshmallows and rainbow dyes and juice pouches, they multiplied every day.

I now have neon pink everywhere. Fluffy blankets, giant throw pillows shaped like unicorns, and tiny pink shoes at the door. And then there's the glitter. Everywhere.

Also, I'm pretty sure I went into the locker room today with a Barbie doll in my gym bag. When I found it on the floor after removing my gym clothes I stuck it in my locker, and the rest of the team laughed at me about it. Joke's on them, really. It looks kind of cute there. And it reminds me of Gabby. There's nothing weird about that.

The longer they are in my apartment, the more I forget what life was like without them. We have a natural routine, and it isn't the uncomfortable, stifling thing that I thought family life would have been. If I'm being completely honest with myself, I feel guilt for not knowing and doing this sooner. I should have reached out. I should have never let Sami go— wait, where did that come from?

Sitting on the bench, I follow the line changes while I wait on equipment managers to get my replacement stick. The guys have been welcoming, but I still don't feel like a part of the team yet. I want to. I've been busting my ass to get Elliot to warm up to me like we used to but he's not having it.

"Blackwood, are you going to skate today or ride the damn bench?" Elliot's words echo through the empty practice rink, and I watch as the rest of the team slowed their own drills to pay attention to us. Gritting my teeth, I get up.

"Here's your twig, Blackwood." The equipment tech that ran to get me another one ran up, panting.

Elliot wants me on the ice? Cool, here I come. I throw a leg over the boards, my blades gliding on the fresh ice, skating straight at him. I slide to a stop, throwing fresh snow up against his pants, and grin at him. If he wants to be a hardass on ice, fine. But I don't have to put up with it.

His eyes look down at the melting crystals on the navy material, before looking up at me.

"Seriously? What are you, in Mites again?"

I shrug. "You wanted me on ice, you got me."

He grunts and rolls his eyes at my insolence, and I can't quite find it in me to stop.

"Can you pretend to be a grownup who has his shit together for one practice session, Blackwood?"

"Can you quit riding my dick like an ugly stripper, Moxley?"

"I should kick your ass for the way you treated my sister," he growls at me, giving a jab to the center of my chest, not enough to throw off my center of balance but enough to be serious. Oh, he wants it to be like that today.

"Jesus, Mox, will you get over your bullshit for once? If you want to throw punches let's go. You're being ridiculous about this."

His eyes go wide, and I'm aware of everyone

around us going quiet and watching. They're always watching, waiting for this exact thing to happen…and now it is.

He throws his stick, the carbon fiber shaft clattering off the ice, and strips his gloves. His helmet is next and he's staring me down like he's going to rip my head off.

Fine.

I toss my own gear down, throwing my hands up into a defensive position.

"You know Sami's going to ask what the hell happened, right? We're going to have to tell her about this."

"It will be worth it," he growls, tossing a right hook toward me.

# Chapter 50
# Sami

Why, why, why, does Kane have to be so damn easy to live with?

He has completely readjusted his lifestyle to let us in. He had Gabby's room painted a shade of pink that will probably never get covered back up again no matter how many layers of primer they use next. The scheduled grocery delivery started including Gabby's favorites. Like, he's actually trying to be accommodating for us. He had the movers put my things in the guest room beside hers so we'd be comfortable.

He's surprisingly attentive and I don't know what to make of this.

I expected animosity, a "You stay on that side, I'll stay over here," separation of goods. But he's making it…easy.

We have settled into a routine, where every night he's free we sit at the dining room table, do Gabby's school work with her, and then he takes her to bed and reads her a bedtime story. He's so involved, and every time I hear him making the voices for the characters, my heart aches. If only I had told him sooner. If only I had given him a chance to have this. We could have had so many more story times, and family dinners, and shared support during appointments.

Did I make a mistake? No, I mentally shake myself. I did what I thought was right at the time. I can't blame myself for the past.

I walk into the kitchen, hoping some tea will calm my racing thoughts. We can only move forward. Breathe, I tell myself, pouring hot water over the teabag.

"Samantha, are you out here?" Kane's voice comes from the hallway, and I have to wonder if Gabby fell asleep on him.

"In the kitchen," I call out, setting my mug down and walking toward him. "She didn't make it very far in the story, did she?"

"Nope, I didn't even get to finish the chapter. We'll start it over tomorrow." He looks past me into the kitchen. "Tea?"

"Yeah, I hoped some chamomile would get me ready for bed."

His eyebrow quirks at me. "Stressed out, are you?"

I roll my eyes at him. "Of course I am. I'm always stressed."

He nods, walking past me to pick up my mug. "Come on, wife, let me take care of you."

"What are you doing? Hey, that's mine!"

"I know," he says. "You're going to go drink this while soaking in the master bath. It has jets."

"But that one's in your room…" I start and he freezes mid-stride.

"I know. But you need it. Now, go get your things, I'll start the water for you."

Without another word, he walks away.

In my lifetime, I've seen him in different levels of growth. He wasn't much to look at in his awkward phases. Kane standing on his own, self-assured and cocky/confident, is enough to make your heart race. Finding Kane on his knees, sleeves rolled up, and testing water temperature for your bath is a whole different story.

And that is how I find him. Bubbles dripping along his forearm, a light sheen on his forehead from the steam. Lord have mercy, this could stop your heart.

"Here you go. Remote is over here," he says, pointing to the bamboo table, and the white square beside my mug. "When you're done, help yourself to the steam shower if you want." With a grunt, he gets up and starts to walk out of the room. "Enjoy yourself, Samantha."

I don't even have the breath to give him a "thank you" before he shuts the door between us.

Maybe – just maybe – he was right.

I stayed until the bubbles were gone, and my fingertips had gone pruney. Whoever designed his bathroom needs a raise. The shower was heaven. And did I end up staying way too long under the spray? Maybe.

Walking out in my sleep shorts and tshirt, near boneless in my relaxed state, all I can think is that I could have never accomplished this level of relaxation at our townhouse. And knowing that Kane knew what I needed? It's a skill he used in college, and clearly hadn't lost.

Some day, he has the potential to be a great partner to someone.

# Chapter 51
## Kane

I made a strategic error.

I didn't think about the fact that the bathroom would share a wall and sound carries. So much for luxury penthouse apartments having soundproof walls. I can hear everything.

Hearing her on the other side of the wall from mine is driving me crazy. She's not even doing anything, except for singing some off-key pop song, and I can hear the pipes in the wall. But I know she's in there. Under the water. Naked. Using my body wash and shampoo maybe, because I didn't see her bring it in with her.

Shit. Stop that.

I walk out to the living room to the bar. Even still, I can make out the soft drumming of the showerhead, and whatever high notes she tries to hit.

She's just your roommate. She's off limits. Get your mind out of the gutter.

"Damned neanderthal," I mutter, pouring myself a drink.

I just have to put on my game face. We shared a house before, it's not the first time that I've heard these sounds from her before.

It's just the first time that I am intimately aware of what she looks like and what she's doing, and I want to be in there with her.

Groaning, I stalk into the kitchen, far enough away that I can't make out anything. Moving her into my place was probably the best and worst decision ever. This is going to kill me.

"Elliot will skin you alive if you defile his sister again, even if she is your wife," I mutter at myself. Sipping at the whiskey again, I focus on the burn and not Samantha.

My wife.

Shit, stop saying that!

# Chapter 52
## Sami

Don't get me wrong. I know what all Kane Blackwood has to offer, and he's not doing much to hide it. Waking up in the morning to see him in the kitchen, building his pre-workout smoothie in gray sweatpants should be illegal. However, it's a small price to pay, I suppose. Today after practice we're having a first appointment with him and Gabby's team. We've had dozens of appointments, conferences with her care team, even meetings with Elliot on hand, but this one makes me more nervous than the rest.

This morning, there is no pre-workout smoothie, gray sweatpants wearing Kane in the kitchen. There's just Kane, in jeans and a henley, pouring coffee into my cup as I walk up.

"Morning. Here you go," he says, as he taps the cup closer to me. I take it with a smile, feeling the heat in my palms.

"Thanks. Are you ready for this?" I point at the binder on the counter, the one that I use to keep all of her current treatments straight.

"Maybe a little nervous, but it could always be worse." Gabby trudges in, rubbing sleep from her eyes as she walks to the fridge. "Hey, Gabby, want me to make you something?"

She mumbles a no, taking a small juice bottle over to her blanket on the couch. She's scared, I can tell, but trying to play it cool.

"I'll go talk to her," I start to say, but Kane's large palm on my wrist stops me.

"Let me?" I nod, watching him walk off toward the couch with her. She's curled in her favorite blanket, zoned out on a video on her tablet, but I see her glance up at him as he comes around the couch, setting his coffee cup on the table. "Can I sit with you?"

"It's your space," she mutters, trying not to take her eyes off the screen.

"It's your space, too, and I don't want to make you uncomfortable here," he returns, his tone soft. "You're nervous about today, aren't you?"

She stares him down, before breaking eye contact. "Maybe."

"It's okay, you know. Did your mom or Uncle El ever tell you about my very first home game in college?"

"No," she replies, drawing out the "oh" while she side eyed him. Suspicious. She can't figure out where he's going with his conversation, and to be honest, neither can I.

"Okay, so. You've been to our games before. Picture this." He holds out his hands laying out the scene for her. "Biggest crowd you've ever seen at that point, and there's people everywhere. You know? I was nervous. I'd never played in a crowd so big, ever. We're dressed but waiting to go on the ice, I've got a bad case of the rumble guts, and your uncle, genius that he is, tells me to drink milk to settle my nerves. Before skating."

"Mom gives me warm milk to go to sleep sometimes, makes sense." She shrugs. "So you go get milk?"

"Yep, I hunted down one of the concession stands that had some in the kitchen. Chugged the whole carton and felt a little bit better, so I headed out for warmups. But that's not the end of it."

"No? What happened next?"

"I skated warmups, stretched, all of that. Then I lined up for the anthem."

"That's it?"

"Nope. It was all good until they got to the line about 'bombs bursting in air,' and I blew chunks, right on the blue line. We took a penalty for delay of game because they had to scrape the ice and run the Zamboni again."

I had to bite my lip to keep from laughing at the story. It was one of the first times I had watched him play, and it was the talk of campus for weeks afterward. Gabby giggles, and it's infectious.

"That was kind of dumb, but funny. How embarrassing, and everyone saw you do it?"

"Oh yeah! For the rest of my season they tried to call me 'Milk Carton,' but it didn't quite stick. But you know what?"

"What?"

"I wasn't nervous after that."

I could see her tilt her head and look at him. "You want me to chug milk and hurl?"

"No, that's not the moral of the story."

"What is the moral of the story?"

"Everyone gets nervous, even dumb jocks like me. Sometimes we just have to get out of our own head to make the nerves go away. What part are you nervous about? Let's build a play strategy like before a game."

"How?"

"Like this," he says, picking up his tablet case from the coffee table, flipping the case around and holding the digital pen over an app, with the layout of the rink. "So, over here we have your uncle Elliot," as he writes a 68 on the blue line. "And I'll go here," as he writes a 57 on the same line, to the right. "Your mom can go here," he writes a 34 in the circle behind Elliot.

"Why is she number 34?"

"Being the younger sister, the guys called her half-pint, so she was always 'half' whatever. Half of 68 is —"

"Oh! 34! I get it now. Where's Aunt Ronni, and what number will she get?"

"We'll put her over here on D, and how about 67 because it's close to 68?"

She nods in agreement, and he continues.

"Who would you want in goal? Bishop?"

She nods, taking a sip of her juice.

"You're here, at center." He puts a "1" in the center position.

"Why 1?"

"Because you're Number One, always." He taps the pen on the opposite side of the ice. "Over here, we're going to have all of the things that make you nervous, and we're going to figure out how to get past them and score, so we can win."

My heart stutters as I realize what he's doing. He's making a visual representation of her support, as well as her fears, to work through them. It's unorthodox, but I can see it working. She leans in close to him, pointing to the positions, and whispering what goes where. He nods as she speaks, and scribbles a letter or shape at each position. Together, they draw out diagram paths between our "team," and the worries on the opposing team. While they are distracted, I sneak a picture of them, huddled close over the play, and send it in a text to Ronni.

Is he really using a play board to work with her? She texts back.

Exactly, I reply.

That's really sweet of him. He's trying!

I start to type a "no he's not" but stop. She's kind of right. Shit. He really is making an attempt. I am amazed at how accommodating he's been. Keep it together, girl, I think to myself as I shake the thoughts loose.

He's just trying to be a good host, I tell her before continuing to watch them interact together, their heads close together as they huddled over the tablet. Their mannerisms were so similar, it was no surprise that they shared DNA. It was heartwarming that he dropped his playboy bachelor life to let her in.

I know he's been trying with me but I just can't let him get close. We set the ground rules, we're sticking to them. Even if watching him act like a real father figure is tugging at my heartstrings. It's just an act, I tell myself, as I look back at the phone.

"It's just temporary," I whisper to myself as I type the words to Ronni. I have to remind myself, we aren't really here and we aren't an actual family. This is just to keep us safe.

# Chapter 53
## Kane

Watching Sami managing Gabby's care is like watching a general strategize a war.

Sitting across from her at a table, with the care team around us, while she fires off question after question, plotting out the next couple months of treatment has me gobsmacked. I've always known that she's wicked smart, but to see it in action.

I'm supposed to be paying attention to what is going on because I'm legitimately years behind, but all I can see is her in her mama bear glory and I'm just here, watching from the bench.

I feel a weird sensation in my chest at that. She's been here, taking notes, doing research, and keeping this ship afloat alone. And I've been where? Hanging out with frat boys and partying the whole time? My gut flips. I should have been here. I should have known. I should have…

"Kane? Did you have any questions?" Sami is looking at me expectantly, and I get the idea that this wasn't the first time my name was said.

Pull your shit together, Blackwood.

"No," I responded. "Let's get started ASAP."

I walk out of the meeting with appointment dates and procedure notes, but I couldn't repeat anything I had been told. I traveled home in a daze with Sami, letting her drive my car because I couldn't even begin to concentrate beforehand.

Having this responsibility on me was making me anxious. What do I do now? How do I just leave after all of this?

The answer was clear: I couldn't. And even more disturbing for me, I didn't want to.

# Chapter 54
# Sami

The truce between me and Kane has been…refreshing. Yeah. That's a good word for it.

We have settled into a nightly routine, where he takes Gabby to her room and they read together for a bit before bed. It's the cutest damned thing, watching him trying to be small on her bed while she explains the specific details of a book that only she seems to remember. Listening to him read the books with character voices tugs on my heart in ways I shouldn't trust, but I can't help myself.

If I didn't know any better, I'd think I actually…like him?

That's all it can be, though. I can't trust him with my heart. The last time took forever to heal. I'm scared to death about what would happen if I let myself go.

I absolutely cannot let myself fall in love. Not in love with him anyway. Ever.

Trevor will put me straight, I know he will. He can't lie to me.

"You're being kind of hard on the guy, don't you think?" Trevor shoots me a look over the ceramic lip of his latte.

"The only good thing to come out of him was Gabby," I shoot back, picking up my own cup.

"However, he has been really good the last little bit."

"Do tell."

"You should have seen him before the appointment, Trev. Gabby was so nervous, and he like, worked with her through it. He got down on her level and they talked it out. It was adorable."

"So he's not totally useless."

"No, he's not. and he's been…nice."

"Just nice?" he asks, eyebrow arching in disbelief. "Is that the best word you can come up with?"

"He's been a perfect gentleman. Holding doors, taking care of dinner, being helpful."

"There's a 'but' in there somewhere," Trevor mutters. "I recognize the sound of it."

"I can't get attached this time, though."

"Can't? Or won't?"

"Is there really a difference? He broke my stupid heart in school and I can't let it happen again."

Trevor's green eyes narrow on me, scrunching up his face a bit, like the words he needs to say taste bad.

"Sam, babe, hear me out…"

"No."

"What do you mean, no? I haven't even said anything yet!"

"I know what you're going to say, and no."

"You are living with this fine-ass man who is apparently worshiping the ground you walk on. You're going to say no to that?"

"What other choice do I have?"

"You have the choice of enjoying what you've been blessed with! I don't know what deity is smiling upon you, girl, but I'm jealous as fuck. He's putting in more work than I would have given him credit for initially."

"Did you forget that this was a temporary arrangement?" I snark back at him, without heat.

"Did you forget that you actually enjoyed his company before?" Trevor counters, grinning. "Or did Gabby get delivered from Ebay?"

"Etsy. She's a one-of-a-kind, original, hand-made."

We both laugh, but I can't keep up the energy. I sigh, resting my chin on my hands, elbows on the table.

"But I still don't know what to do about him."

"You two already have a connection, and it may not be a bad thing. See where it goes. If nothing else, you're going to enjoy the journey."

# Chapter 55
# Kane

I'm trying really really hard not to say or do something stupid like "I'm in love."

I can't be.

Sonofabitch, I wasn't supposed to fall in love with her. Again. Or had I ever actually not loved her?

Do I still find her hot? Abso-fuckin-lutely.

Does she still rile me up and piss me off? Damn straight.

But…love? Nah…not that. I absolutely can't.

I ran out of the apartment today without my shoes on to escape because oh my God she was in the kitchen making breakfast and the sunlight just hit her and I lost track of everything. I forgot how to breathe. I think I saw my future pass before my eyes. What the hell is that even?

But I can't tie her down to me. I couldn't do it the last time, how could I ever consider burdening her with my bullshit again?

Absolutely not. No way.

Besides, Elliot will probably kill me if I break his sister's heart—again. He's hellbent on stuffing his knuckles in my face any time he can, and I can't say I really blame him.

I was the reason she almost didn't finish school.

The reason why she has been making decisions alone all these years.

I'm the one that destroyed everything.

All I can do is try to do right by her moving forward, and if that means keeping her away from me, then so be it.

My fingers trail along the little black box that I've kept tucked in the back of my closet. I had every intention of making her my wife back in school. I even scraped together enough money from my leftover stipends to go over to the mall and pick out whatever ring I could have possibly afforded. It wasn't much, but it was supposed to be hers.

I don't know why, after this long, I still have it. Maybe it's my punishment for all of my mistakes before. All I know is that every time I go to leave it behind somewhere, I just can't do it.

It's a little box of what should have been.

# Chapter 56
## Sami

I am a strong, independent woman. I can do scary and hard things. No one has the power to make these decisions for me without my permission.

So why the hell am I trying not to hurl at the dinner table because Kane is sitting beside me? Good God, girl, get a grip!

"Samantha, are you okay?" His deep voice broke into my panicked thoughts.

"I'm fine."

My reply was raspy, barely a whisper.

Gabby has gone to bed earlier, exhausted after a day of school, leaving us both at the table alone. Together. There is a lot to be said about tension that comes from unspoken words. I can't deal with it, but I also can't say the words that are on the tip of my tongue.

"Are you sure? You look kind of panicked. Did something happen at work? Did the doctor call?" he freezes, staring at me with wide eyes. "Is Gabby okay?"

I shake my head. "No, nothing like that."

"I'd like to think we can still talk things out like grownups. You know you can tell me anything."

"It's not that serious, I'll be fine."

"Samantha," he starts picking up his fork. "Who

do you think you're fooling with that? You are stressing about something, and I want to help. What's wrong?"

"You're going to laugh at me."

The corner of his mouth kicks up as he tries to hold in a smile. "I promise I won't."

Fine, he asked for it, I think. Taking a breath, I turn toward him.

"This has been nice. Comfortable. I thought we would have a harder time acclimating to this living situation."

"It's not the first time we've done it, so of course it's comfortable. But I don't think that's all you're struggling with."

"I'm worried we're going to get too comfortable. You said this wasn't going to be forever, but what if we did. No deadlines, just rolling with it?"

"Samantha, are you getting attached?"

"You're tolerable," I say, laughing.

Oh my god, please don't pry.

"Just don't get attached. I'm no good for you."

"You are a good guy, though. Don't sell yourself so short."

He shakes his head, a sad smile on his face.

"You need someone solid, stable, who hasn't spent the better part of a decade partying. Someone responsible. I'm not the one."

"And what if I think you are?"

The words slip out before I can stop them. We both freeze, eyes locked on each other. My heart thuds dangerously close to my throat, but I hold still, trying not to run away in a panic. It's too late to take it back now, and even though I'm scared to death of what he'll say, I feel lighter getting it out.

"You don't actually mean that," he says softly.

"No, I'm pretty sure I know what I meant. You're underselling what you bring to the table."

# Chapter 57
## Kane

This woman is going to be the death of me.

Staring me down, daring me to say a word to the contrary, she won't give me an inch. A shiver creeps down my spine as I realize that she's not willing to let me slink off into the shadows, leaving her to find someone better. She will not take that at face value.

"I'm not a knight in shining armor, Samantha. I will never be the one who comes in and saves the day on a white horse." Raking shaky fingers through his hair, he added, "I'm more likely to burn it all to the ground and leave you standing in the ashes."

"You know I hate it when you call me that. It sounds like you're trying to put something between us."

"And if I am?"

"Knock it off, Kane. You're not that bad of a guy and I'm saying I want you to stay."

His head shakes.

"I'm not a good guy, and I've made mistakes. I can't—"

"You can't do what, Kane? You can do whatever you want! You are Kane Fucking Blackwood."

"I'm not someone you want to keep around. As much as I love you—"

He freezes, mouth hanging open as he realizes

what he just said.

I love you.

I blink, processing what is between us.

"You…love me?"

Cursing, he turns away from me, leaving my question hanging heavy between us.

"Samantha, please," he whispers.

"Say it again."

"Don't, just — don't—"

"Don't be a damned coward, Kane. Say it again.

"I—I love you. Fuck it, if I'm honest, I never stopped loving you."

I crumble. The walls I've worked so hard to keep up, keeping this as a strictly transactional relationship, disintegrate at his words. A tear runs down my cheeks as I look at him with fresh eyes. He didn't do this to be intentionally mean, he did it because he wanted to keep me safe. Even if it broke us both in the process.

Without thinking, I launch myself bodily at him, flinging my arms around his neck, and rejoicing as I feel his strong arms wrap around me, holding me safe. Just like he always did. My lips met his in a clash of lips and tongue, a total wave of feelings and emotions that we kept away from each other for so long that were now free.

"Kane, I need—"

"I know baby, I know," he murmurs back, as he walks me back toward my bedroom. Our bedroom, I don't know anymore.

Every time he touches me, it feels like the first time. Sparks fly. My skin tingles and burns under him. Chemistry has never been a problem with us, but this is a whole new level now. He growls in impatience as the door doesn't open behind me. A giggle escapes me against his lips, turning into a gasp as he turns the knob and walks in, kicking the door shut behind him.

# Chapter 58
## Sami

I can hear my alarm going off somewhere in the room, but it's not on my nightstand. Sami is curled into my side, hugging my arm, and I can feel the pins and needles in my fingertips. Her ass is pressing against my dick and I'm reluctant to move, but that god awful chirping is annoying the shit out of me.

"Too fucking early," I grumble as I try to shift out from underneath her. "Sami, babe, I need my arm back."

I hear her grumble a "don't wanna" before she rolls away from me, taking the comforter with her. My jaw clenches as I feel the cool morning air against my extremely naked ass. Well, I'm up now, I think to myself as I move to sit up, looking around the room for where I left my phone. I think I hear the obnoxious hunk of plastic coming from where my pants are tossed against the closed door. Untucking the sheet from where it's crumpled at the foot of the bed, I wrap it around my waist lightly and shuffle that way. It needs to shut the fuck up before I –

"Kane?" A soft tapping on the door makes my heart jump into my throat. "Kane, have you seen my mama? She's not in her room."

Fuuuck.

I look over at the sleeping form of her mother, the woman who doesn't apparently hear through walls. "Sam," I whisper-yell, walking back toward the bed as quietly as I can. "Samantha, get up!"

"Huh?" She pulls the blanket away from her face, her eyebrows drawn together in annoyance under her wild hair. "What the hell—"

"Kane?" Tap-tap-tap.

"Oh shit," she mouths at me.

"What do I do?" I whisper back.

"Go help her! I have to get dressed!" her words hiss between clenched teeth as she throws the blanket and scrambles to pick up her clothing, nearly falling over in her rush to grab everything.

"One moment, Gabbi, I'll be right out," I call through the door, throwing a pair of sweatpants and a random t-shirt on before walking to my door. I drop a glance back at my ensuite, watching Sami dive behind the door before I turn the handle myself. "Hey, Gabbi girl, good morning."

"Hey, Kane. I don't know where Mama went, and I'm going to be late to school. I got dressed already, but I need help with breakfast."

"Well, we can't have you starving," I agree, pulling the door shut behind me. "Let's go see what I have in the kitchen. My trainer stopped by with a new protein powder that I'm supposed to be able to make pancakes with, and I have a secret bag of chocolate chips."

"Chocolate chip pancakes are my favorite!"

"Sounds like we've got breakfast covered, kiddo. Come on, you can stir."

She climbs onto a barstool, pink Converse swinging in the air over the rungs, and watches patiently for me to get situated. I pull out the ingredients and set them in front of her, her eyes sparkling as I pull out the fresh bag of chocolate chips from a shelf.

"Have you made pancakes before?" Her question reminds me that it's been most likely years since I've taken the time to do this.

"I have, but it's been a while. I used to make pancakes for your uncle Elliot and your mama when we went to school together."

"Oh yeah, I heard about that. You played together." She pulls a banana from the fruit basket on the island and begins picking at the sticker on it. Funny, I think, I've done the same thing since I was a kid. "So, is that why Uncle Ell is mad at you?"

I freeze. "What's that?"

"He's mad at you. I heard him tell Mama he'd punch you in the nose again. Can't you make him pancakes to make him happy again?"

"I think this is bigger than pancakes can fix, short stuff. It's okay. We'll get there eventually, right? Otherwise, Christmas is going to be real fu– I mean, freaking awkward."

We settle into a relaxing silence, she eats her banana while I flip the next pancakes. The feeling is relaxing, and much more comfortable than I would have expected domesticated bliss to be.

"What are you two up to here?" Sami pops around the corner, her hair damp and loose around her shoulders, an Ice Wolves hoodie and jeans on.

"Mama! I knocked on your door but you didn't answer, so Kane said he'd make me breakfast!"

"That's nice of him, baby. Sorry, I guess I didn't hear you over the shower." She walks into the kitchen, dropping a kiss on the top of Gabby's head before moving to the coffee pot. I can feel her right beside me, like static. "She conned you into chocolate chip pancakes?"

"It wasn't much of a con job. She needed breakfast, and I needed my protein. It seemed like a win-win. You want some?"

"Sure, thanks, Kane."

We lock eyes for just a second, and I can feel my heart thud against my chest. God, this woman is going to be the death of me.

"Anytime." My attempt at sounding casual fails hard, and it sounds all husky and weird to my ears.

"Don't burn them! Kane, look out!" I look down at the skillet and curse, looking at the round pucks that I've incinerated.

Sami tries to hide a giggle behind her coffee cup, but the pink in her cheeks gives her away. She knows what just happened.

"Those were the test ones. The next ones will be perfect."

"Sure," Sami mutters to herself as she walks away, a sway to her hips that wasn't there before. Tease.

Pouring fresh dollops of batter in the pan, I try to shake off the feelings. We don't have time or room for feelings, I remind myself as I make a point of ignoring the woman sitting at the counter watching me intently.

# Chapter 59
## Kane

Reconciling with Sami is one thing. Getting back in Elliot's favor is another. I should have known that I would have had an uphill battle with him. Even during our first season together as kids, we didn't really become friends until almost the end of the playoffs. And then we were inseparable. We even went to college together simply because we could.

And then Sami happened.

Sure, she had always been around, tagging along at our games, practices, and even when we hung out on our own. When it was time for her to come to college too, we automatically agreed that she should come stay with us and we could keep her safe. It was just like being at home again until our senior year happened.

I saw little of her between workouts and her own activities, but when we moved back in the fall, she wasn't just that little sister hanging out with us. She was gorgeous. I couldn't keep my eyes off of her. We had studied together for years and now, just smelling her shampoo made me feel things I shouldn't about my best friend's little sister.

There's some unspoken rules that teammates have. I don't know who thought this dumb shit up, but it's just hockey bro code. Never step on the team logo in the locker room. Don't give a girl your team sweater unless you mean it. And most importantly: Don't fall for your teammate's sister.

And I did. Hard.

I'm pretty sure he knew something was up when I spent less time with him. He wasn't happy about it. But dammit, I felt bad. I was the one that tag-teamed scaring off her potential dates. No one was good enough for her. Hell, I didn't think I was good enough for her, but there I was. Sneaking out on dates with her, stealing kisses in the tunnel when she waited for both of us, sending texts back and forth under his nose.

Knocking her up before burning every bridge I had between me and a Moxley.

I owed him a proper discussion. One that has been years in the making, I know.

"Moxley, you got a minute later? I need to talk to you," I say, trying to keep my voice as soft as possible.

"Why?" The question is perfectly valid, but it still has me gritting my teeth to hold back a smartass comment.

"Jesus, are you going to make me do this in the middle of the rink?"

"Where else did you want to 'do this thing,'" he counters, a mocking tone at the end. Knowing him, he had his face pulled in some stupid face when he said it, too, but I wasn't about to look at him. The assholes we play with would see something up and circle like sharks sniffing out blood.

"I was thinking of trying to get in at Nico's, Roby said it had awesome steaks."

He snorts, shifting his stretch so he had to look my direction. "You would never get in. They don't know you." He sighs, sinking into another thigh stretch. "I'll call them and see if we can get in tonight. Fine?"

"Fine. And thanks. I mean it."

I get back on my skates, then glide out onto a warmup lap.

Fighting for # 57

Dinner with Moxley is a tense affair. He did one better and pulled a favor to open early, so we sat in an empty dining room, hair still dripping from our respective showers, staring at each other while the waitstaff rolled silverware at the bar.

"You wanted to talk, so…" he trailed off, waving a hand over his salad like he could pull the words from me.

"I wanted to apologize."

"I'll need to you clarify that statement."

"I'm sorry about Sami, and how I left everything, and Gabby."

"You know you almost broke her, right? She liked to pretend I didn't actually know, but I had a feeling something happened between the two of you."

Staring hard at him, I ask, "How? What…how?"

"I didn't really put it all together until she said she had to go to Vegas. And then when you came here, that sealed it. But you two were close, and then after you left she was just broken." He took a sip from his water glass before continuing. "And then when she found out she was pregnant, she wouldn't say anything. She kept that secret to the very end."

My head dropped into shaky hands, and I ran my fingers through my damp hair. I didn't expect being a single mom in college to be easy on her, but I also didn't expect this much destruction left in my path.

"I wish I would have known. I don't know if I would have stayed but, maybe I would have tried harder."

"Is that supposed to make me feel better about you being a shit human?"

"Dammit, Moxley, I'm trying to apologize. I made some big mistakes."

"No shit, Sherlock. I was the one that picked up the pieces behind you, helped keep her in school, while getting my career off the ground, and then went to every doctor's appointment throughout the whole journey. I was the one that stayed with her through two days of labor. And where the hell were you? Doing body shots off a stripper? Real Father of the Year material there."

"She never told me. I — well, I don't know if I could have stayed, but I would have tried to help."

"Why Vegas? You went to the first team that looked at you and completely threw our plans out the window while you were at it."

"If I tell you, you can't tell anyone. I mean it. I could get in serious trouble here."

"You mean worse than seven years of back child support on a pro player's contract?"

"Yeah. Worse. And for the record, I've put that total into an account for Sami. I started setting that aside the day she left me hung over in the Hard Rock." I shift uncomfortably under his gaze. "I'm not trying to be shitty to her. I hope you get that."

"So what is so bad, then?"

This is it. This is the moment. Maybe he'll understand and can help me keep Sami safe after all.

"You know that my upbringing was, um, unorthodox."

He nods. He was around for a good chunk of the BS my parents put me through. He was the one who saved me more than once from going without.

"I ended up owing some money to someone for my sperm donor. It was a bad situation, and they had the potential to really hurt me and anyone attached. They threated you and Sami, specifically, because they knew I was close to you. I cut ties. It seemed easier. Go away, go where they couldn't get me, and I wasn't around you."

"Kane, we could have helped." His tone is soft, one I had heard before, the one he used after I came over in the middle of the night to escape the drunken fight at home. "Surely we could have done something, you wouldn't have had to do anything…" His words hang heavy in the air. "What have you done?"

I shrug, thinking about my past sins.

"Nothing major. I haven't killed anyone, it's not that serious. Mostly threats, delivering funds back and forth, collecting money from bigger people. I might have roughed up a few guys before." I pause. "I haven't had to do that in a bit, though; I'm too visible now to be a heavy, but it happened a lot in the early days."

"Jesus," he whispers, eyes wide as he just looks at me.

"I'm not proud of it. Any of it, really. To be honest I wouldn't have gotten into any of this if it wasn't for Rick." I shudder, thinking back to the man who was supposed to have been my dad. "He got in deep and used me as collateral. The longer I worked off his debt, the harder it was to get out."

"Of all the fucked up, hairbrained ideas to come up with, this has to be one of the most off-the-wall. What the hell?"

"I didn't say I was proud of it, or that I didn't regret it. But it happened. I'm trying to cut the last ties and moving here was the biggest step."

"So, moving in with my sister is a safe bet?" His gaze narrows as he talks, he's not convinced.

"I'm trying. But I have to be honest with you."

"Don't let me stop you," he responds on a sarcastic laugh.

He's going to punch me again.

"I'm in love with your sister."

"About damned time you figured that shit out."

"I mean it, Elliot. I love her. I don't think I ever stopped, really."

"So what do you intend to do about this, genius? You're the one who put yourself in this mess."

"I don't know. I really don't know. I mean, for the moment, she's keeping me at a distance."

"As she should. Last time she let you close, you bounced. Coward."

# Chapter 60
## Sami

He loves me. Kane Blackwood said "I love you" to me.

I'm scared shitless about it.

"Could I really trust him to stay around? It was so easy for him to disappear the last time. I can't do it again."

"Sami, it sounds like he's actually trying. And he's a whole grown man this time, not just a kid fresh out of school. Maybe he's learned a thing or two." Trevor's voice distorts through the speakers as he tries to reason with me. "What happened the other night?"

"He said he loves me. That maybe he never stopped loving me."

"That's adorable," he sighed through the phone. "Would he really do that if he planned to leave?"

"He told me the morning before I caught him with the puck bunnies and he disappeared, Trev. I don't know what to think anymore."

"What is your gut telling you right now? Be honest."

Pulling up to a red light, I think about that. "I think maybe I still did, too."

"That you what? Still love him?"

"Yeah…"

I let the word trail off as the light turns green and I

move forward again. I have to admit that there was a certain amount of appeal in getting back together with him again. Our chemistry has always been off the charts. But how much of that was just the forbidden fruit being sweeter? We were never affectionate in public, always hidden.

"You know my thoughts on it, and you have my support either way. If you want to make a serious go of this, do it. If you feel like he's best at a distance, do it. But if you keep that man for yourself, I fully intend to be your Man of Honor when you marry him."

"Technically, we're already married," I argue, turning into the parking garage.

"You deserve a big celebration with all the cake and fun. Don't sell yourself short."

"Okay, fine," I grumble, pulling into my assigned spot.

"I have to run to this meeting, love. Keep me posted!"

I hang up the call and step out into the concrete enclosure, a cold chill going down my back. The parking under the building has always given me the creeps, but it was a secure lot with good lighting and cameras. Gathering my bag, I reach for the fob to lock up behind me.

"Hey, aren't you Samantha Moxley?" a woman's voice asks from behind me.

"Yeah, that's me—" I reply, turning to the voice. I see a dark-haired woman in a leather jacket standing beside an SUV two spots down.

And then she punched me, and the world went black.

# Chapter 61
## Kane

I feel raw and exposed, and for the first time in a long time I'm not looking forward to coming home to see her.

Elliot read me the riot act throughout dinner. I expected it. My steak tasted like cardboard under the stress, and pulling in the garage, I see Sami is home already, her little SUV with Elliot's "#68" sticker in the back window. I groan, dropping my head against the headrest, feeling my pulse throb in my temple and my eyelid twitching in time. I don't even have a minute to pull myself together before I see her.

Ready or not, here I come.

Meditative breathing in the elevator to our apartment, and a last breath before opening the door—

—To nothing. Alarm still set, no one in the house. The box on the wall chirps insistently at me, warning me that if I don't do something soon, it will wail at me.

Frowning, I type in the code and look around. Where else could she be? That is definitely her car in the garage, but why isn't she in here? Her phone goes right to voice mail. I call down to the concierge to see if she went there in person first, but they had no record of anything after her swiping her keycard at the garage gate an hour ago. Did she go to Elliot and Ronni's?

Calling Elliot first made sense.

"No, I don't even have a text from her asking to come by. She would have checked to see if we were home first," he answers, which does nothing for my nerves. "Are you sure that was her car in the garage?"

"Yeah, it's hers. It was in our spot and it has that Ice Wolves sticker on the back window. Plus, the front desk said she swiped into the garage earlier. It doesn't add up, but I don't want her to feel smothered."

"I can keep trying her phone…wait!" he yells. "She's on my phone plan. Or we have a shared plan. She's used it to find me before. We can find her that way."

"Where is she?" I bark at him.

"Calm down, it's looking. It takes a second." My heart pounds in my ears as I wait. "Hey, it isn't showing in the building. Actually, I don't know why she would be there—"

"Where?"

"On the riverfront, where the casinos are? She's there."

My gut knots, and I slide down the wall behind me as my knees buckle.

"I think I know where she is. Or who she's with, anyway."

"Who? Do I need to call the cops-"

"No. No cops. I'll get her. Send me the screenshot of the location to be safe."

"Kane, I'm not sure if it's a smart idea to go after her in that area."

"Elliot, let me fix it. I got her into this mess. I'll get her out. Promise."

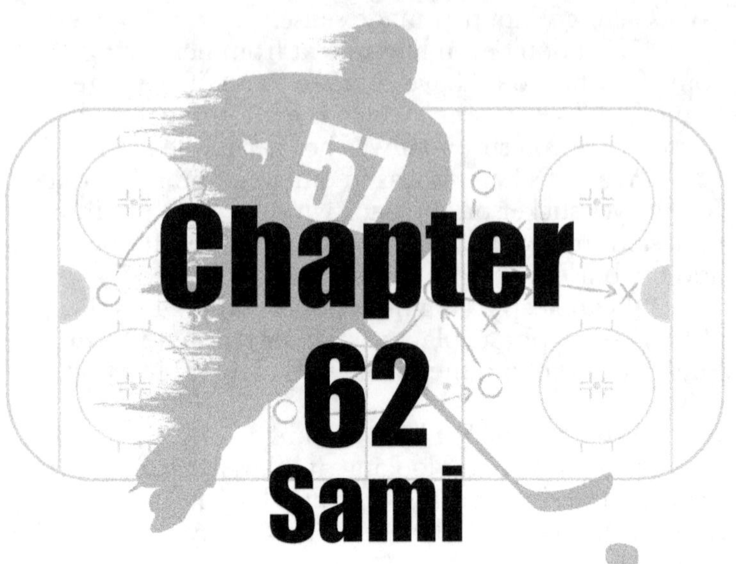



My head is pounding worse than after the frat parties. I feel like I'm missing out on an important detail here, but I can't get my brain to focus.

What happened to me?

Wisps of memories come to me. Talking to Trevor on the phone. Pulling into the garage. Gathering my belongings. Someone saying my name.

A woman. Dark hair. She punched me.

Where am I?

My heart pounds as panic sets in. Am I in the same building? Did she take me somewhere?

"Wakey wakey, Samantha." That woman's voice breaks into the fog and panic in my head.

It sounds like the same one from the garage, but I can't be sure. I crack open an eye with a groan.

"Who-who are you?" My words slur, my tongue too heavy to form words.

"I think you know. You took my man."

"What? Kane said he was single."

"My uncle got him for me and made him take me out because I wanted him. He's mine, bitch!" She slaps me hard across the cheek, fireworks blasting before my eyes.

They'll never recognize me at this rate, and no one

knows where I am. I don't even know where I am.

"Where am I?"

"Nowhere important. We need to talk. You need to tell Kane to leave you alone and come back to Vegas with me. Now. I'm not staying in this shithole of a city with him."

A giggle bubbles up before I can stop it. "What do you know about hockey contracts? He's stuck here."

"I can get anything I want. And I want him out of here. I'm taking him whether you agree to it."

I don't know what is scarier, that she thinks the commissioner will agree to this or that she believes anything she says can happen, or that kidnapping me was her idea of a good plan.

Be cool, Sami, just relax, stay calm.

My phone vibrating in my pocket distracted me from the woman. They left my phone on me? What the hell?

Please, please be Elliot and Kane, I think, as I feel the vibration stop and then start again. Gabby is at school and I'm supposed to be picking her up. Waves of nausea hit me, imagining how worried my baby girl will be if I'm not there. Hot tears make me squint. I refuse to let this woman see me cry.

# Chapter 63
## Kane

My chest aches and all I can think is I'm having a panic attack.

I told Elliot no cops, but I have a feeling he's going to do it, anyway. He always did what was best, where I always tried to work my way around the problem on my own.

I'm independent to a fault, I was always told.

He left to pick up Gabby from school, and I left to go find Francesca. I should have known that she would do something extreme some day. I mean, who has their uncle demand dates of someone, anyway?

I sat at a small table in a coffee shop near the riverfront, watching for Francesca to show. She wouldn't deny me. I knew her too well. She would ignore the fact that I shouldn't be this close to where she was and come running because I called.

Because she would think I wanted to see her. That I finally "came to my senses" about us together.

I watch as she comes in, flicking her hair over her shoulder against the breeze. My jaw aches, teeth grinding against each other as she walks toward me with a sway to her hips that should be appealing.

"Kane," she purrs, holding out her arms to me as though I should get up and hug her.

"Francesca," I growl, refusing to get up.

"What, no love for me? How disappointing," she pouts, sliding into the chair across from me.

"You wanted to talk, let's talk."

"I don't know if I like your tone." She reaches across the table from me, taking my drink and sipping from it. She grimaces when she realizes I got my usual, a black Americano. "I don't know how you drink this, it's horrid."

"Black and bitter like my soul," I counter sarcastically as I cross my arms across my chest. "Where is my wife? What have you done, Francesca?"

"We're not talking about her. She doesn't matter."

"She does matter, and dear God, kidnapping? What the hell were you thinking?"

"She was in my way, Kane. I removed her from the situation and she's no longer in my way."

Pressing my lips tight, I contemplate how to word this.

"Is she—Did you—"

"Don't be so damned melodramatic. I didn't hurt her."

"I have doubts." I grumble, looking around the room. "What do you want from this?"

"I want her to leave you alone. You're supposed to be with me."

"So if I tell you we're together, you'll let her go? Just like that?"

"You'll need to give me more than just pretty words. But yes. Leave her and I'll let her go. I'm not totally horrible."

"As if I haven't worked with your uncle. I want proof." There's no way she'll just let Sami go, not if she's aware of the situation and the people around her. The more you know, the more likely you'll end up in a ditch somewhere. I shiver, thinking of the consequences.

"Uncle didn't tell me you were so melodramatic," she pouts, staring at me. "Not that serious, Kane, really."

"No? You just kidnap people for fun? Come on, Francesca."

She shrugs a shoulder under her designer Italian

leather jacket. "Fine. It could be worse, but it's not. Now let's go take care of this so we can go on a date."

Jesus Christ, she's ridiculous.

I get up and gather my things, sliding my coat on my shoulders. Tucking my hand into the interior pocket, I make sure that the pink case of Gabby's phone is still hidden with my wallet.

# Chapter 64
## Sami

I have to get out of here, and I don't know how. That woman left what feels like forever ago, leaving me with a couple of goons that looked like they would fit on the defensive line in a beer league somewhere.

My phone stopped buzzing a while ago, and while it might have meant nothing in the long run, it hurt my heart to think they weren't still trying. I missed my baby girl. I missed Elliot, and worst of all, I missed Kane.

He's the reason I'm in this mess, but my heart cracked thinking that he would never know how I felt. It's taken me forever to come to terms with it, but damnit, I love him. I can't explain why I do, considering our history, but I love him.

And I may never get the chance to tell him.

There is commotion outside the room, and I look up in time to see that woman again. She's back, glaring at me like she did before.

"I still don't know what he sees in you," she spits at me, her tone cold and bitter. "Like, what is this? You dress like a bum. Oh and you saddled him with a kid! What kind of underhanded bullshit is that, anyway? I can give him a better life than all that."

I bite my lip, refusing to talk. I can't give in to her taunts, I don't know what she'll do to me.

"Untie her," she orders the goons sitting by the door. "She has a guest."

"What?" I croak.

The scariest guy comes over to me, yanking hard on my bound wrists. I fight to keep from whimpering as my shoulders scream. I hear his knife flick open behind me, and cool metal against my wrists as he slices through the zip ties. Groaning, I pull my aching arms in front of me, grateful that I can feel the circulation returning to my fingers.

"Stay put," he grunts, holding me down by my shoulder. As if I would go anywhere, I don't know where I am or who is on the other side of the door.

She turns, going back out the door, and I can hear her talking with someone. A man. As she comes back in, I fight the panicked urge to scream because walking in behind her, looking calm as can be, is Kane.

My Kane.

I gasp, sobbing, as he makes eye contact with me. Cool, calculated eyes lock on mine. I don't know what he's doing, but he's giving me nothing to work with.

# Chapter 65
## Kane

I could hear the pounding of my heart in my ears, seeing Sami sitting there with her head bowed. Her puffy, red eyes locking on mine, and I felt my knees buckle.

She's here because of me, and this is all my fault.

My feet feel heavy as I walk in behind Francesca, watching her motion to her thugs to let Sami go. My breath freezes in my lungs until I watch her stand on shaky legs before they shove her toward us.

"Kane, give her your keys. She can leave. You're staying."

"Excuse me?" Sami and I echo each other, turning to shoot her an incredulous look.

"Did I stutter?" she arches a brow, looking at the two of us. "She can go. But you're staying with me."

"What–" Sami starts to say, and I cut her off.

"Fine. Just let her go."

Two of Francesca's guys grab Sami by the elbows, pulling her up from the chair.

"No, Kane, don't do this!" Sami begs, trying to pull her arms out of the grip they have on her. My fists clench at my sides, I want nothing more than to punch the shit out of their faces for daring to lay a finger on her, but I have to look at the big picture. I need her to get out of here.

They drag her in front of me, and I hold out the keychain to her.

"Samantha, I need you to do this, okay?" I take her trembling hand in mine, laying my car keys in her palm. "Take the car, and go home. I'll take care of this. I promise."

"No, Kane, she—"

"I know." I can't stand that I'm interrupting her but I have to tell her. "I need you to go home. Don't worry about me. I just want you safe. Trust me."

Tears fall down her cheeks, and for a split second, I wonder what the odds are I can get both of us out at the same time.

"But you'll be here."

"I know. I lo—"

"Okay, that's enough," Fracesca's shrill voice breaks in. "Kane, go sit down. Take her outside. I don't care what happens to her."

I keep my eyes trained on Sami's as she's dragged out of the room, screaming my name, her eyes wide in fear. I mouth "I love you" at her before she passes out of my line of sight.

"Happy now, Francesca?"

"Very. Now go sit down."

# Chapter 66
## Sami

I refuse to look at my phone until I climb into his car, the engine roaring to life under me and peel out of the lot as though the hounds of hell are behind me. I don't know why she let me go, but I'm not sticking around to let her get me again.

Even though Kane is still in there.

He made it clear I was to leave, don't come back. But I can't just leave him there. What if she hurts him instead?

As the worn down industrial area morphed into downtown, I pulled off into a grocery parking lot, breathing deeply for the first time since before I got out my car earlier. My numb fingers desperately fumbled in my pocket for my phone.

Gasping, I looked at the screen. So many missed calls and messages from Elliot and Kane.

Elliot: Stay safe, baby sis, I love you. I have Gabby.

Kane: I love you. I love you. I love you.

Ronni: Hey girl, the school just called. Do you want me to go get Gabby?

Ronni: Oh nevermind, Elliot just called. We've got her!

Kane: I swear I'll fix it all. I'll never forgive myself for this. Just remember, I love you. I love you I love you

I love you.

Tears flood my eyes, every feeling and thought of the last day hitting me like a tidal wave. All my fear, my love, the pain, all of it overwhelmed me. Choking on sobs, I let it all go.

He loves me. He's sacrificing himself for me. He let that woman trade my freedom for his and I just left him there. I left him there!

My gut churns, and I barely open the door before heaving. I'm a snotty, red-faced mess and I'm in the middle of God knows where.

I have to call for help.

Wiping the sour taste from my lips, I take shallow breaths through my nose. In, out. I press Elliot's name, and he cuts off the first ring.

"Sami? Are you okay? Where is Kane?" He barks rapid-fire questions at me, before I can even attempt to answer.

"I'm…I'm…"

"I'm coming to get you. Stay put."

I pull my phone away and end the call, before calling 911.

"911, what is your emergency?"

"I…I think my friend is in trouble. I was taken and I'm not sure where exactly I am."

I can't focus on the conversation. My thoughts are all over the place. I hope Kane is okay and we can recover from this afterward.

Elliot rips into the parking lot, tires squealing, and barrels through the line of first responders to get to me.

"Sami! Sami, oh thank God you're okay!" My giant of a brother crumpled before me, his knees buckling as he landed in a heap on the pavement at my feet. With a sob, he leaned forward and crushed me in a hug. "Kane said he would get you out and not to call the cops but I had to, Sam, I just had to, I'm so sorry!"

"It's okay, I'm okay, It's— but El, he's still in there."

Elliot's eyes lock on mine. "What do you mean, 'he's still there,' Sam? He stayed?"

I jerk my head up and down. "She said he had to stay with her if she let me go. So he did, he told me to go and take his car, and he stayed."

Sitting back on his heels, his eyes unfocused a bit. "Stupid fucker, if he gets himself killed now, I swear…" He shakes his head, looking up for the officer nearby. "Hey, our friend is still at another location. Here," he says, holding out his phone, showing the officer the screen.

"What are you doing, El?"

"He's in the app."

"How…?"

"I knew he'd do something stupid. But also, I hoped we could use it to find you. Just in case."

# Chapter 67
## Kane

She's gone. Sami left, just like I told her to, and now I'm here in her place. I can only hope that she makes it out to Elliot. Maybe they'll send help from me, maybe they won't. I'm not sure if I deserve it after everything I had put them through.

Francesca stares at me from across the room, her arms crossed across her chest, eyes narrowing as I return her look. I will not let her intimidate me into shit.

"Well, you have me. Now what?" My taunt echoes off the concrete walls.

"I told you it didn't have to be this way."

"We're past that now, Francesca. I told you no, you didn't accept that, and so you decided kidnapping is a perfectly normal response to being rejected. So again, what the hell are you going to do now?"

"Quit yelling at me," she pouted. "You're supposed to be my boyfriend."

Taking a deep, cleansing breath through my nose, I will myself to calm down.

"Francesca," I say, pausing. "I can't be your boyfriend because I'm married."

"The hell you are! I checked, Uncle said you were single! He said I could have you so who the fuck did you marry?"

I just stare back at her. Watching, waiting for the truth to sink in. Her eyes widen, her cheeks taking on a scary shade of red.

"No, you didn't…I should have killed her."

"Touch her, and I'm liable to forget that I'm usually a gentleman."

"You wouldn't dare."

"Try me."

She screams, her shrill voice echoing off of the walls around us.

"You asshole," she bellows at me, swinging her pistol at my skull.

"That's gonna put me in concussion…" I trail off, the words feeling sluggish on my tongue.

"Police! Freeze!"

I can just make out dark shapes swarming into the room before my vision fades to black.

# Chapter 68
## Sami

"Where. The Hell. Is my husband?"

The words come out in a staccato, and I'm trying my damnedest to not throw things. Around me, doctors and nurses are scattering to complete their checks of patients and, hopefully, Kane as well. I peek into gaps in doorways, desperate to lay my eyes on that man.

A nurse in green scrubs stands in my way, blocking my view into another curtained area. She holds her hands up like a stop sign and starts, "I'm sorry, ma'am, you can't be back here—"

"I'm looking for my husband. Kane Blackwood. He was just brought in." My words are breathy, broken by my ragged breaths sawing in and out of my lungs.

"Oh, my apologies. Let me take a look at the intakes, okay?" She sits down at a computer, typing in a few words.

"Sam…Samantha?"

I turn so quickly I nearly lose my center of balance. Laying on a gurney, gauze on his forehead and bloodstains on his shirt. My breath whooshes from my lungs and I go weak in the knees, relief flooding me at seeing him alive.

"Kane, I…" I whisper, before stumbling over to him, throwing my arms around his shoulders.

"Hey, shh, it's okay," he murmurs, pulling me closer. A large, warm hand runs slowly up and down my spine, and murmurs sweet sounds in my ear. "I'm okay, you're okay, we're good."

"But-but you were—"

"I probably have a concussion. Not the first time, you know? I just need to get some scans to make sure." He drops a kiss against my temple before looking at the two nurses on either end of the bed. "Hey, any chance she can at least walk with us? Just to be safe?"

I latch onto his hand, walking along beside him until we get to the radiology lab. The tiny circles he drew on the back of my hand calmed my nerves, and slowly I felt everything calm down around me. He is okay. I can see him and talk to him. Gabby is fine. I can talk to her, and she's safe with Elliot and Ronni.

"Did— did I hear you call me your husband? In public?" His voice is soft, only for my ears.

My eyes drift shut, flashbacks of my outburst in the lobby assaulting me. I nod, biting on my lip nervously. His dreamy gaze brightens, a grin breaking out on his face.

"Fucking hottest thing you've ever said, babe," he whispers, so soft that I almost don't make it out over the humming noise and activity around us.

"Really?" Skeptically, I side eye him. "That's what you're going with?"

"Yeah. You have no idea how good it sounds from you."

My cheeks grow warm, and I can't help but smile back.

"You definitely need to get your head checked, because you're talking nonsense."

"My head's just fine, we're getting ready to find out. You'll see."

"Sir, it's time to go back," a nurse says apologetically, unlocking the wheels on the gurney.

"I'll be right back, okay? Love you," he says, dropping a kiss on the back of my hand before he's wheeled behind the double doors.

# Chapter 69
## Kane

Coming back home after Francesca's ordeal has felt like a fever dream. Maybe I'm still unconscious, just dreaming about Sami at my side. I've wanted it for so damn long. Maybe my dreams are my own delusional reality.

She doesn't let me out of her sight. Ever. If I walk to the kitchen, she's getting me a plate. If I go to take a shower, she's outside the door when I come out. She won't admit to it but she's not sleeping that great and I'm constantly waking up to see her watching me, eyes wide.

I need to talk to her about it. We both have some scars left from the ordeal, but mine are just more visible. She's shaken, my strong and unbreakable girl is fragile and unsure now. It's unforgivable.

Concussion protocol blows, and sitting at home with no screens and brain rest works my last nerve, and listening to Sami running around the kitchen waiting on me is the absolute last straw to break my patience. To hell with this.

Leaning against the island in our kitchen, I watch her, all chaos and frenetic energy, as she mutters to herself. She's working herself to the bone and it shows in the dark circles under her reddened eyes, and the rumpled shirt she stole from me last night.

"Samantha," I call out softly, just to catch her attention.

She screams, the mug that she carried flying out of her hands and shattering on the tile floor, shards of ceramic and waves of tea going everywhere.

"Shit! Sorry, I'll clean it up," she cries, dropping to her knees with a towel.

"Stop, hey, come here," I say, cursing at myself for scaring her. "It will be okay. I need you to stop and sit down, you're working yourself into the ground and I'm worried for you."

"I'm sorry, I—"

"Stop apologizing." I hold her quivering chin in my hands watching as her eyes water. "You've been through a lot here with me, but I need to help you, my love."

Her eyes drift shut, her eyelashes releasing the tentative hold on the teardrops, leaving a wet trail on her cheeks. I wipe at them with my thumbs.

"I'll be fine, I just—"

"Samantha. Let me help my wife." She shivers, her eyes still closed. "Are you going to listen to me?"

"Maybe."

# Chapter 70
# Sami

They say, "If you love something let it go. If it comes back, it was meant to be."

I know that it's meant for letting someone go and provide distance, but I can't bring myself to let Kane out of my sight. It's ridiculous, I know it, but I'm so damn scared that if I so much as blink, he'll go away again.

Francesca will come back for him, even though we saw her hauled off in cuffs.

He'll take back the Ice Wolves contract and go back to Vegas, away from this domestic thing we have.

Trevor is on his way to the arena to see me, and I hope he can talk some sense into me. I'm in the Trainer office like I always am, but I have an eye on the door to the locker room.

Quit being such a damn stalker, Samantha, I yell at myself in my head.

My phone buzzes, distracting me from my doorway vigil, and I see Trevor's name on the screen.

Trevor: I'm getting coffee. Want one?

Me: Yes, please! I need all the caffeine today.

Trevor: Did you sleep at all? Wait. Don't answer that. Come out here so I can lecture you properly.

I sigh, tucking my phone away. Kane is headed out

for practice, where Elliot will be with him the whole time. He's safe, it's fine. I let my team in the trainer office know I'm stepping out for a minute, and head outside the arena to the coffee shop where I know Trevor will be waiting.

Sure enough, by the time I make it there, Trevor is sitting in a booth, looking just slightly overdressed in the crowd of Ice Wolves jerseys in his tailored pants and loafers, a wool coat hanging behind him.

"Sami, babe, I got you your usual," he greets me, standing to give me a light hug and air kisses as always. I smile, returning the gesture before taking a seat opposite from him. He settles gracefully into the seat, ankle crossed casually at his knee, and long fingers steepling over his latte. "Care to tell me why you need an economy sized gallon of coffee to get through the day?"

"Can I get halfway through this before I answer that?" I cringe. I should have known that of anyone, he would ask. Elliot has given me the look like he would ask, but he won't make conflict. Trevor has no such compunction.

"Sam…" His words trail off ominously. "I'm concerned for you. It's not healthy for you to stay up for hours watching your man sleep, and then trying to watch him work, too. Maybe you need to consider talking to someone like the detective said."

"I will," I promise. "I'm just worried."

"They cleared him to skate again. There's nothing physically wrong with him now."

"I know. But last time I let him out of my sight, I got him back with a concussion and a bleeding head wound."

"Babe," he looks at me over the wire rim of his glasses. "That's called trauma. I worry about you because you can't be Supermom to my niece if you're sleep deprived. Got it?"

"I know. And thank you. I mean it."

"If you meant it, you'd go home and get some sleep. Let that man of yours do his job, and you talk to who you need to talk to."

"Yes, Mama," I chirp back, rolling my eyes at him.

"Anyway, what's new with you? I feel like we haven't talked in ages. Are you still seeing…" I trail off drawing a blank.

"Oh, heavens, no," he replies, screwing his face up. "Apparently, his ex came back. That's fine. He was a horrible date, anyway."

"I'm so sorry."

"I'm not," he counters on a laugh. "Babe, life is too short for crappy books, food, and dates. Move on to something more enjoyable and stop wallowing in what makes you miserable."

"What are you trying to say there, Trev?"

"Besides the fact that I've had to DNF two books in the last week, and a wilted salad at lunch?"

"You asked if I was good, now it's my turn. Are you okay?"

"I'm fine. I'm just a bitter bitch," he muttered. "There's a severe shortage of cute, single guys in the area who don't have more issues than Vogue."

"We'll have to fix that," I say, nodding my head. "We can't have you bitter and alone."

"Samantha?" Trevor and I both shoot a look at the new voice, and see Kane standing in the doorway of the coffee shop.

"Kane! Come meet Trevor!" I say with a smile. Finally, I think, I can get these two in a room together!

"Kane, Trevor is my best friend, and also one of Gabby's favorite people."

"Gabby thinks everyone is her favorite," he counters, smirking. I recognize that face, he's had it on the ice before, usually right before he starts a fight.

"I'm aware. She also picks her favorite based on who has what snacks. She's sneaky like that," Trevor interjects, holding his hand out. "It's nice to meet you, finally, Kane."

I watch them closely as they shake hands. Kane is clearly eyeballing him to gauge if he's a threat. And Trevor is looking him up and down like he's a piece of cake.

"Trevor," I hiss under my breath, earning a slight eyebrow raise. "Not your kind."

"Pity." He smirks, giving Kane's hand one more

pump before nodding at the extra chair. "Come sit with us. Can I get you something?"

Kane's gaze screams he's suspicious of the kind gesture, but asks for a water all the same. I breathe and watch them move to sit before lowering myself back into my chair.

"Sorry, Sam, I didn't know you were meeting a friend. The intern said you went out for coffee so I thought I'd catch up to you." Kane's voice is soft against my ear, before he places a kiss against my temple.

"You're good. I've been hoping to get you two in the same time zone at some point. It's important to me you like each other."

"So, you're the best friend," Kane starts, his tone factual. Trevor nods in response.

"And you're the baby daddy," Trevor returns.

"No. I'm the husband," Kane corrects, and my heart flutters in my chest.

Trevor's beautiful cheshire cat grin lights up his face.

"Glad to see you're coming around to owning that. Sami deserves it."

"Okay, if you two aren't going to kill each other, Sami is going to the bathroom," I snark, getting up.

Kane snags my hand as I circle behind him, pulling me up short. "We'll be right here when you get back. Okay?"

I nod and move back down the hall, allowing the silence and soft jazz music soothe my irritated nerves.

# Chapter 71
## Kane

My eyes stay on Sami's back until she's out of my sight, and then I turn to Trevor.

If I thought Elliot was going to be the hard one to convince, I was sorely mistaken. But I'm not going to let this man know that.

"I suppose I should thank you for looking after her and Gabby while I was," the words trail off. I don't know how to finish that thought.

"Not a problem. There's not a lot of 'looking after' with her, anyway. She'd rather do it all herself. You know how she is."

I nod, remembering how strong-willed she had always been, and how she still is. We definitely know the same woman, that's for sure.

"How long have you known her?"

"We've been friends since our sophomore year. We had some classes together and the rest, as they say, is history. You've known her since high school?"

"Before that, I think. I knew Elliot more than Sami, really. We played hockey together, and she had to tag along, usually bossing us around about finishing the workouts or warmups that Coach instructed us to do."

"That sounds like our girl," Trevor laughed.

I feel like I know him, somehow. Our stilted

conversation going smoother until Sami returns to us.

"Oh good, you didn't kill each other while I was gone," she snarks, coming back to the table to sit between us. "Everything good?"

"Just great, love," Kane answers, leaning over to squeeze my thigh in reassurance. "I think Trevor and I will end up being great friends."

"Really?" she says, looking at me with narrowed eyes.

"He's not that bad, really," Trevor chimes in. "You should keep him around."

I can see her visibly relax, her shoulders sagging in relief. Trevor and I continue to share a conversation, finding similarities between us. No wonder Sami likes him. As we talk, I feel Sami lean heavier against my side. Her eyes are closed, and she's resting precariously on my shoulder.

Running a hand over her thigh, I murmur, "Babe, I think it's time to get you home, love."

She opens her eyes slowly, to focus on mine, and sighs. "You're probably right."

"Kane, get our girl to sleep some tonight, okay? She's dead on her feet."

"She can hear you," she grouses, frowning at us.

# Chapter 72
## Sami

Elliot might kill me for this one, but it's what I need to do. I have the original annulment documents in my purse. And I'm heading to meet Elliot and Kane at the arena. Crazy as it sounds, the two of them have become best friends again recently. Walking into the wide open arena, preparing to face them for Family Fun Day on the rink, I consider what I'm planning to say. All I can do is hope that we can walk away from this with our hearts unblemished.

"Sami, you made it!" Ronni calls across to me, and I smile in return. Her relationship with Elliot has been beautiful, and her visits with Gabby have really been a morale boost during some of her worst days.

"Yeah, I figured I'd let Kane and Elliot have some solo Gabby time before I busted up their party," I say, grinning. "Are you heading to the rink now?"

"Working our way there," she confirms, and I look to see her coworker and friend, Jessica, coming around the corner as well. "Are you okay? You seem nervous."

"It's been a minute since I've been on skates, really," I fib. I'm not going to let anyone know what really has my gut churning. Can I do this? Can I tell him the truth?

"No problem, Kane won't let you down."

If only she knew.

I follow her to the tunnel entrance, the whisper of skates on ice and the laughter of children echoing off of the concrete walls. One of the giggles I could be hearing might very well be Gabby. Butterflies launch in my stomach because if Gabby is out there, the odds are high that so is Kane.

I don't know if I can pull this off. I'm a strong, independent girly, but what if he turns me down? What if he says he already sent in his copy? What if…

"Mama!" Gabby's voice breaks me out of my negative spiral, and I smile at her.

"Don't run in your skates, baby girl!" Kane's deep voice is soft, guiding her without being critical.

"But it's mama and she's so slow!" Gabby stops walking to turn toward Kane, where I see that she's wearing a miniature of his own jersey. She has never, ever worn someone else's number. It's always been Elliot's. Their faces go out of focus, and I wipe away the beginnings of tears. My little family – and we are a little family, the three of us – and I might be tearing us apart if he doesn't feel like I do.

Kane looks me over, his forehead wrinkling as he looks at my face. I shake my head, hoping he picks up on my wordless "please don't ask," so we don't mess up Gabby's outing for her.

"Hey, Gabs, how about if you go with Aunt Ronni and tell her what we did to Uncle El's laces."

"Yeah! Hey Aunt Ronni!" Gabby waddle hops on her blades toward Ronni, who continues down the tunnel with her. Ronni peeks back over her shoulder at me and I flash her a smile and a thumbs up, so she won't worry.

Kane walks up to me slowly, like he's afraid I'll run. Or worse, cry.

"Hey," he says softly, cradling my head in both his large hands. "What's wrong?"

"I didn't want to say it here. Or, not out here, in the tunnel, I had a plan."

His dark brow quirks. "Okay, keep going."

Sighing, I try to break eye contact with him. Not that he'll let me, the man is all about connection.

"Fine. I wanted to ask you something. And show you," I wiggle out of his grasp, pulling my tote around so I can pull out the tan envelope and hand it to him. "I wanted to show you this."

A tilt of the envelope and I know he can see the logo of the lawyer I had talked to shortly after our marriage. He takes the envelope from me, carefully pulling the prongs through the hole. I can sense the moment he stops breathing, reading the header on the paperwork.

The paperwork that would render our drunken Vegas marriage null and void.

His eyes lock on mine again, and he swallows hard. Without even looking, I know what he's reading. It's confirming that I'm asking for an annulment, reverting back to my legal name, even though the only things with Samantha Moxley-Blackwood on it are the original marriage certificate and the credit cards he had made for me.

"I didn't– I didn't think we were going to–" His words are broken, eyes staring sightlessly at the white pages in front of him.

"Kane," I start. "I want us to shred them."

The envelope falls from his numb fingers, white sheaths of paper slipping free against the rubberized floor.

"Oh thank god, I thought you wanted to go through with it!" He wraps me in his large arms spinning me around, shoes crumpling the pages. "Wait," he stops, looking out to the tunnel. "We can go shred them now, in Ronni's office. I'm sure she'll let us. But first, I want you to have this."

Thick, shaky fingers dig in the front pocket of his jeans, hidden under the hem of his practice jersey, before he pulls out a box.

A very distinct, recognizable ring box.

"Is that– you mean– oh my god."

"Samantha," he starts, "I should have done this years ago. You're the only one who I could ever love so deeply, and you are, without a doubt, the only one who has ever had my heart." A peek down the tunnel, and he added, "Well, now one of two. Our girl has had me wrapped around my finger since we met."

Choking on a watery sob, I nod in agreement. "Yes, I–"

"Let me finish," he starts, looking down at me with a mock stern expression. "As I was saying, you're the only one who has ever – could ever – own my heart. It's always been yours. I want us to stay, just as we are. My wife. If you'll keep me." Kneeling before me, ring box balanced carefully in his large hand,  he asks, "Samantha, will you marry me?"

"Yes, please, always," I whisper, falling to my knees in front of him, shaky arms wrapping around his neck.

With a jolt, he steps away from me. The sudden separation has my heart racing in panic.

"What's wrong?" I whisper, bringing numb fingers up to my tingling lips.

"We have to go. Now." Snatching my hand away from my lips into his warm grasp, pulling me toward the rink. "Ronni! Ronni, where are you!"

Ronni pops around the corner, concern etched on her face. "Are you two okay?"

"Toss me your office keys! We need to shred something."

"Right now?" she asks with a tilt of her head. "We can go up after skating."

"Nope, we're doing it now. Just give me your keys, please."

She reaches in her pocket, puling out a single key on a hockey stick keychain.

"Do you want me to come with–"

"No, just give me the keys. Now please." His tone is sharp, his voice echoing off the walls.

Ronni stares, open mouthed, and tosses the keychain underhand to him.

"Wait, you're not...Kane, not in my office you don't!"

"We'll be fast!" Kane laughs, running the opposite direction, with me in tow.

Breathlessly I run after him, to head into our future.

# Epilogue
## Sami

### Two years later...

"Gabby! Let's go! We're gonna be late!" Kane's voice bellowed up the stairs.

"Come on, Daddy's right. We gotta go, Gabby girl." I give one more pass of the can of hairspray over her curls, then life away a stray thread on her shoulder.

"Is this dress okay, Mama? I don't know if it's right."

"It's beautiful, baby girl. Now, let's go downstairs."

At the top of the stairs, I pause so she can go down first. Looking down from the landing, I take in Kane leaning against the railing, his all black suit tailored beautifully, and the light glinting off of his watch as he tilts it to see the time again, before he looks back up at us. A slow grin warms up his face as he watches Gabby descend the stairs in front of me.

"There's my beautiful girls," he says, holding out a hand for Gabby, who jumps from two steps up to stand beside him.

"You like my dress?" Gabby asks him, holding out the edges of her skirt and giving a partial twirl.

"Give me a twirl," he says, holding out his hand to guide her in a pirouette on the slick bottom of her dress shoes. "I love your dress."

She grins widely, then looks up at me. "Come on, Mama! Let's go!"

I step down the stairs carefully, and he takes my hand gently in his.

"Hello, wife," he murmurs, leaning in to place a soft kiss by my ear. "I love that color on you."

"I know you do," I whisper back at him, grinning as his eyes darken. "Come on, we're going to miss the dinner service at this rate."

"Nah, Ronni would wait on us," he counters, walking us toward the front door and out to the waiting car.

"You haven't witnessed her laying into Elliot because he's thrown off her schedule, then," I laugh.

"I have. But the thing is, she likes me and I don't do it very often. Besides, we have the guest of honor, right?"

"Right!" Gabby chirps from beside us, skipping along to climb into the opened car door. "Let's go! Aunt Ronni said there was cake!"

I let Kane help me into the car, making sure the end of my train is tucked into the car before climbing in beside me himself.

Two years ago, this night went a lot differently. I interrupted Kane's big romantic gesture at the same event with my impromptu trip to come clean with Kane. This time? He's here by my side. We're attending the event as a family, and Gabby is presenting the auction for Elliot's charity. It's wild how things can change in such a short period of time.

My eyes drift over to Kane, a soft smile on his face as he looks over at us.

"You're thinking awfully hard over there, Blackwood." His attention focuses on me, eyebrow raising as he questions my statement.

"I used to attend these things solo, or with random people. This is already the best night ever."

"It's always good when things work out," I say, leaning my head against his shoulder.

"I'm so glad you found me again," he murmurs against my hair, kissing it softly.

Looking over at Gabby, in her cloud of silk taffeta,

and playing on her phone, I have to agree. We may have had a long journey to get here, but we finally made it where we should have been.

"I love you, Mrs. Blackwood," he whispers, dropping a soft kiss by my ear.

"I love you more, Mr. Blackwood," I reply, giving his thigh a squeeze.

This is it. This is what I've always dreamed of. The man I love by my side, my daughter, and the knowledge that we are stronger than any challenges life may throw at us.

This is the forever worth fighting for.

Here we are again! "Fighting" was definitely fighting with me, so this labor of love had real blood, sweat, and tears in it this time. I have so many people to thank for getting me here.

First and foremost: That tattooed man I married. He's the one who would hint that I had a book to write if I tried to avoid it. My behind-the-scenes support system. We may never see him at a book signing with me, but he's the one wrangling me back behind the keyboard. I love you so much!

Rose, you knocked it out of the park again! Thank you so much for being patient when I said Fighting would be in your inbox by a certain date, and then promptly destroyed the manuscript a month beforehand.

Paige, my alpha baby work wife! Where would this be without you? Thank you for the support, hearing my dumb ideas, and redirecting me when I thought about burning the whole thing down with fire.

My family, who are always behind me. Sorry about the F-words!

The Romance Riot. What can I say? Thank you to this merry band of misfits who have provided bookish support and accountability when I needed it! Cheerleading from y'all has definitely helped keep me going.

To everyone who has picked up a copy of my books, reviewed, shared with friends: Thank you so incredibly much. It truly does take a village to keep an author going, some days.

# About the Author

Eden Knox is a sports romance author who lives in Ohio with her herd of animals and her veteran husband. She can often be found cheering for the Blue Jackets and Penguins, during hockey season or the Pittsburgh Steelers during football season.  When she isn't tormenting her fictional hockey team in The Sin Bin Series, she can be found lurking at the public library with a long list of book recommendations.